MURDER ON THE AISLE

MURDER
ON THE
AISLE

——

Edward Gorman

St. Martin's Press
New York

Library of Congress Cataloging-in-Publication Data

Gorman, Edward.
   Murder on the aisle.

   I. Title.
PS3557.0759M786 1987   813'.54   87–4438
ISBN 0–312–00623–3

First Edition

10 9 8 7 6 5 4 3 2 1

To Loren D. Estleman,
with respect and gratitude

I would like to thank David Edelstein of
The Village Voice for his help with this novel.

MURDER ON THE AISLE

1 Tuesday: 5:35 P.M.

"You see 'em, don't you?" the cabbie asked.

"Yeah, I see them."

"Around the block again?"

"Yeah, around the block again," Tobin said.

He sat back in the cab and tried to prepare himself for the confrontation he had been avoiding all day.

The cabbie, glancing in his rearview mirror, said, "I always liked you better anyway."

"I'm sorry," Tobin said, coming up through his thoughts as if from deep water. "I wasn't listening."

"I said I always liked you better anyway."

"Me?"

"Yeah. You. I mean better than that partner of yours, that Dunphy guy. He's kind of a snob. You're more like the average man. Like me. That's why I always liked you better."

"Well, thank you."

"My wife always watches you guys, too. She loves it when you get to arguing about a movie. She even tries to predict which ones you'll like and which ones you won't. You know—it's like handicapping horses or something."

"I'm glad you enjoy the show."

"I'm gonna tell her you were one of my fares today and she'll tell everybody she knows. She's like that." He nodded ahead to the Emory Communications Building. "They're still there."

"Yeah. I see 'em."

"They must really want you bad."

"They do."

"Mind if I ask why?"

Tobin sighed. "Well, my partner and I had a little disagreement last night."

The cabbie laughed. "Hey, that's great." Then he said, "I think they've figured it out."

"Figured out what?"

"That you're in the cab."

"Why?"

"They're pointing at it."

"Shit."

"Why don't you duck down? I've had a lot of people duck down in my cabs."

"Great idea. Thanks." Tobin ducked down. He wondered if Roger Ebert and Gene Siskel ever had to duck down this way.

"So you want me to slow down?"

"How about one more time around the block?"

"Fine with me."

"Tell me when I can sit up."

"We're going past now."

"Are they looking?"

"Yeah, they're looking *and* pointing."

"Shit."

"We're past 'em now."

"You sure?"

"Sure I'm sure. You can sit up."

So he sat up. Now, at dusk, Manhattan was alive with Christmas decorations swinging in the chill winds. There were plastic Santa Clauses with light bulbs inside their bellies and little elves with big hammers and reindeer who looked realistic enough to do everything except take a dump.

Then they were around the block again.

"You better duck down again."

Tobin sighed. "The hell with it."

"Huh?"

"May as well just get it over with."

"Really?"

"Yeah. I've got to be inside there anyway in the next twenty minutes to tape a segment. They're going to catch me one way or the other. Why don't you just pull up to the curb?"

"Sure. If you say so."

They parked about a hundred yards down the street from Emory Communications.

Then the reporters started approaching.

Actually, it was only one of them, and the closer the man got, the more obvious it became who he was: Carmichael, from one of Rupert Murdoch's rags. Carmichael, though essentially a gossip columnist, always wore designer combat fatigues. It's a jungle out there.

Tobin sank back and waited.

Carmichael came up with a microphone pack slung over his right shoulder. It might have been a Geiger counter checking for radioactivity. He came up to the rear window and looked in. "How's it going, Tobin?"

Carmichael waited a decent time for a response—all the while locked in a stare-down with Tobin—then rapped his knuckles on the window.

"Might as well get it over with, Tobin. And you might as well talk it over with somebody who likes you instead of—" He nodded over his shoulder and rolled his eyes as if lepers had just strolled by. "Instead of them."

3

Tobin sighed, hit the button for the window to descend. When the electric whirring stopped, Tobin said, "It wasn't a big thing."

"Well," Carmichael said. "It was in a very fashionable restaurant."

"It still wasn't a big thing."

"Tobin, Christ, you decked him."

"See!" Tobin half-shouted. "See! I knew this thing would get blown out of all proportion!"

Carmichael looked embarrassed.

Tobin slumped in the seat. He was wondering how long it took to become autistic. Autism sure would come in handy right now.

"Tobin?" Carmichael said after a bit.

Tobin kept his chin on his chest. "What?"

"You did hit him, right? I mean, you're not trying to deny that, are you?"

"Mhjrygmj." He spoke directly into the woolen scarf he had wrapped around his neck to keep Mr. December from biting him on the ass and all those other delicate places.

"What?"

Tobin raised his chin slightly from the muff of his scarf and said, "I hit him but I didn't 'deck' him."

"You sure?"

"What's the first joke people make about me?"

Carmichael thought a moment. "That you're cheap?"

Tobin grew impatient. "Besides the fact that I'm cheap."

"That you've been married four times?"

"Besides the fact that I've been married four times."

Carmichael looked stumped. "Hell, Tobin, what?"

"God, man, how tall am I?"

"Oh, right. Your height."

"Yes, my height. How tall am I?"

"Say, that's right. You're just a little ba——bugger. Five-four?"

"Five-five."

"Five-five," Carmichael repeated.

"So how tall is Dunphy?"

Carmichael shrugged. "How the hell would I know?"

"His driver's license says he's six-two."

"So?"

"So how could somebody who's five-five 'deck' somebody who's six-two—unless he was standing on a chair, which the restaurant didn't provide me last night, at least not to stand on so I could punch somebody's lights out. You see, Carmichael?"

"But you do admit you hit him?"

"As I already said, I do agree I hit him."

"And you do agree that you two haven't gotten along for quite a while."

"I'll let Dunphy speak to that."

"And it's also true that Dunphy is thinking of not signing on again when his contract runs out after tonight's show, isn't that right?"

"Gee, Carmichael, I don't even need to respond. You seem to have all the answers."

Carmichael said, "You two were roomies in college, weren't you?"

"I believe those were his feet I always smelled, yes."

"And you were the best man at his wedding, weren't you?"

"Yes, and he was best man at three out of my four weddings, too. He would have been at my fourth but he came down with appendicitis, the lucky bastard."

"He was lucky to have appendicitis?"

"I should have been so lucky," Tobin said. "If I'd had some sort of affliction at the time, then I couldn't have married my fourth: the woman who *proved* that

5

Vassar girls are, in fact, descended from a strain of the hunter shark."

"So maybe you'll patch it up?"

Tobin leaned forward, eyes scanning the pinkish dying sky alight with scattered stars. A traffic chopper did figure eights or some goddamn thing above the silhouettes of office buildings.

Then his eyes lowered to street level again and he noticed that the crowd of reporters was beginning to inch closer.

"Tell me," Tobin said, "how the hell did you convince them to let you come up here first?"

"I just told them the truth."

"About what?"

"About your temper."

"What about my temper?"

"Tobin, Jesus, no offense, but when you drink you're an animal."

"I like a little fun with my drinks."

"Does throwing somebody through a window constitute a 'little fun'?"

"Depends on whom you ask, I suppose."

"I mean, you know your nickname."

"I hate that goddamn thing."

"Well, if the shoe fits and all that shit."

"Just drop it about my nickname, all right?"

Then Tobin looked at the reporters again. Now that they'd seen that Carmichael was having no trouble, they had apparently decided there was no reason to let him have the scoop.

"Shit," Tobin said, watching them come up and surround the car.

"Is it true you've sought professional help to try and deal with your temper?" The first question was asked by a guy who might have been a girl or a girl who might have been a guy.

The second question was, "Did Dunphy call you Yosemite Sam to your face right before you punched him?"

There it was. That silly frigging nickname. Yosemite Sam. As if he could help being five-five and red-haired and ill-tempered.

For the second time, he sank back in the seat and let their questions swarm over him.

He should never have pulled up in a cab. A ten-year-old Chevy would have been much better. Might have inspired a little pity.

"Mr. Tobin, is it true your third wife left you when you pushed the dishwasher down two flights of stairs in your town house?"

2

6:18 P.M.

He stood in the back of the theater. He had been about to walk back to his dressing room when the owner of the company that syndicated the show, Frank Emory, appeared as if by magic and blocked his way.

"Why don't you avoid seeing Dunphy if you can?" Emory said. "I think things would run a little smoother that way."

As usual, Emory managed to look both polished and terrified. From his father he had inherited the kind of snotty good looks, now complete with graying hair at the temples, that one usually associates with imperious bank presidents and preppy politicians. Unfortunately, from his mother—Tobin had gotten to know both of Frank's parents pretty well—he had inherited the notion that everything that hadn't yet gone to shit was about to. The clearest evidence of that could be seen in Frank's soft blue eyes. In a head so handsome, they should have looked more confident.

"Don't worry, Frank. I'll go right to my dressing room," Tobin said.

"I'm not taking sides in this," Frank said, giving every indication that he was about to cry.

Tobin put his hand out and touched Frank's arm. Frank was a professional fuck-up. He was forty-nine and had gone through four different businesses, each one of which his father had been called in to bail out from near bankruptcy. His father was in pharmaceuticals and had done very well. Praise the Lord. Emory Communications, however, which owned this video-tape studio and theater and produced syndicated television shows such as *Nashville Calling* (kind of a live version of *National Enquirer* and all about people with names like Ferlin and Jake and Dody), was coming off the worst year of its six years of existence. So Frank Emory looked more shattered than usual. Which was why Tobin was patting him on the arm. Tobin wasn't sure he liked Frank Emory, but at least he felt sorry for him, which was more than he could say for most people.

"Calm down, Frank. I know you're not taking sides."

"He's really going to do it, isn't he, Tobin?"

"He might be bluffing."

For just a moment—no more than a millisecond—you could see that Frank Emory really wanted to believe this. Something like a smile lifted his upper lip. But then his mouth abruptly wrinkled into a frown. "There's no point in lying to ourselves."

"Maybe he is, Frank. Bluffing, I mean."

"You'd understand how much was riding on this if you'd seen the new Nielsens."

"They're in?"

In this business you awaited Nielsens with no less dread than you awaited biopsies.

Frank nodded.

"Well, how did we do?"

"You did fine. You and Richard, I mean. Number-three show in the syndicated Top Ten."

"Well, fuck, Frank, let's go get drunk and feel up some women or something."

"You wouldn't be laughing if you'd seen how the rest of the Emory shows did."

"Bad?"

"Tobin, since the ratings came out this morning, three big markets called in to let me know they wouldn't be renewing at least one of our shows. Philadelphia. Los Angeles. Miami." He called the names off as if they were valiant soldiers slain in battle. "Not even *Nashville Calling* did very well."

"Gee, I thought that show you did on transvestites in country music was interesting."

Frank could only shake his head at Tobin's grim humor.

Around them, grips and makeup men and lighting people moved. The young ones moved quickly and with a certain hostility, not unlike that which Tobin had noticed in the limo drivers. The older ones moved less quickly, and with dull resignation. They knew that the rush didn't matter, that no matter how many things went wrong, shows somehow went on anyway and generally did all right for themselves. Besides, this was the medium that had produced Allen Funt and Michael Landon: It wasn't the sort of thing you had to take really seriously. It was just television and not even network television, for Christ's sake.

"Frank, it's going to be all right. He'll calm down."

Frank said, "There is one thing I'd like to say. I mean, I think we're friends enough that I can say it."

"I know what you want to say, Frank."

Frank raised long fingers splayed in frustration. "Didn't it occur to you what you might be doing to our livelihood here? Weren't things bad enough already?"

Frank was whining. Whining had a way of carrying farther than just plain talking. The crew, young and old, both kind of slowed down so they could get a proper earful.

"You know what you're doing, Frank?" Tobin whispered angrily.

"What?"

"Giving them some nice fodder for the bar tonight. They'll be discussing this till dawn."

"Their jobs depend on the outcome of your contract negotiations, too. Face it. They may as well listen. Every one of us has a stake in this show—Richard, you, me. . . ." He waved his hand at the crew. "Them, too."

Frank didn't say it, but Tobin could already see Daddy waiting in the wings, pockets stuffed with good green cash, ready to bail out his son.

"Why don't we talk about all this after the show?" Tobin suggested gently. Frank was going to hell. He somehow had to get his mind off it. "Why don't you go to your office and have a drink?"

"My wife's in there."

"Good. Give you somebody to talk to."

"She isn't speaking to me."

"Why not?"

"Well, we were having lunch at the club when the waiter brought a phone to my table. I got the ratings over the phone. I didn't bear up well. I—I started crying, Tobin. Right in the middle of the main dining room. With the goddamn snotty waiters standing around and everything. You know how waiters talk. It'll be all over."

"Jesus."

"So Dorothy's pissed. Very pissed. She's back on her *why didn't I marry a real man* routine."

"Then go around the corner, Frank."

"Around the corner?"

"To Delaney's. Have Delaney put you up with an IRA cocktail."

"What's that?"

"You don't need to ask questions, Frank. You just need to drink it. Now go—all right?"

Frank straightened up, thankful that somebody was telling him how to live his life. In his blue blazer and white shirt and yellow striped regimental tie, he was a formidable-looking man. Just as long as he kept his mouth shut. Just as long as you didn't look at his eyes.

Frank had just turned back to the exit door, apparently considering Tobin's advice, when his wife Dorothy appeared from the east wing.

Dorothy's age was kept a secret. She was one of those women who might have been thirty-five or fifty. She was tall, slender, and elegant and spent at least as much money on her blond hair, her red nails, and her tanned legs as the Pentagon did on nuclear submarines. Tobin liked her sometimes, disliked her others. He had never been able to form a final opinion of her.

"Hi, Tobin," she said, leaning in and giving him a Hollywood kiss on the cheek. She smiled and took his hand. Her touch felt wonderful and he decided to like her for sure and for good. "My husband here is all shaken up about what happened with you and Richard last night. But let's try to assure him that everything's going to be fine."

Frank said, "Tobin thinks I should go over to

Delaney's and have something called an IRA cocktail."

Dorothy laughed. "That sounds like something you could have used this afternoon at the club. Did he tell you about it, Tobin?"

"I tell Tobin everything," Frank said. "I always tell him he should have been a priest."

One of the grips came up. "Mr. Emory, there's a call for you."

Frank nodded.

Then the grip said, "Mr. Tobin, Linda said to tell you she's waiting."

"Thank you," Tobin said.

Dorothy kissed him on the cheek again. "Don't worry, Tobin, between your efforts and mine, we'll get my husband to act like a real man someday."

Then he remembered why he *didn't* like Dorothy sometimes. She couldn't resist belittling her husband— even when he had it coming.

"As soon as I'm done with this phone call, I'm definitely going to have one of those cocktails," Frank said. "What are they called again?"

"IRA," Tobin said.

Dorothy drifted back to the east wing, where there was a comfortable lounge. "I'll see you both later."

Frank watched her go. "She's a wonderful woman," he said. And then he smiled at Tobin. "Sometimes."

"You didn't shave very well."

Tobin leaned forward in the chair and looked into the mirror. "No, I didn't."

"But you still look cute." Linda, the makeup woman, laughed. She had a great laugh. A great butt, too.

"Are you sure forty-one-year-old men can still be cute?"

"Sure."

12

"Are you sure that forty-one-year-old men *want* to be cute?"

Linda laughed her great laugh again. "Beats being ugly."

"True enough."

A knock came. This was the makeup room upstairs, where stars of lesser magnitude prepared. Who'd be calling on him here?

"You want me to see who's there?"

"If you wouldn't mind," Tobin said. He felt like a child. She had put a bib on him to protect his shirt from the makeup.

Linda took her great butt (which Tobin watched with a good deal of reverence in the mirror) over to the door and opened it.

The woman on the other side of the threshold caught his gaze immediately. "I just wanted to see if Tobin was here."

Linda knew who she was, of course, and apparently liked her because her tone was very friendly. "Sure, come on in. I'm all done anyway."

Tobin watched the mirror as she came in. She was a suburban beauty. Not the exotic sort you found in fashion magazines but the sort you found in supermarkets pushing a shopping cart and two kids. Freckles. Blue eyes. A lovely if not quite spectacular body. She knew at least something about Emmanuel Kant (she'd been a 3.7 student) and she was perfect company on rainy Friday nights for sharing a joint and listening to old Crosby, Stills, Nash, and Young albums. She got sentimental very easily but it was a deadly mistake to think of her as uncomplicated because she had as many secrets as a movie star's secretary. She had responded to her husband's unfaithfulness by being unfaithful herself. Though she had always been Dunphy's girl, Tobin had known her first (he still remembered the brilliant autumn afternoon when she'd walked into the student union in her fawn-colored suede jacket and her mysterious blue gaze) and loved her first, and so it had made sense that when Jane wanted to have an affair (not to pay Richard back, only so she could have some sense of purpose in her own life) that Tobin would be the man.

"Well, good luck on the show tonight," Linda said as she was leaving.

"Thanks," he said.

"She's sure a nice woman," Jane Dunphy said.

Tobin decided to get it over with. "You haven't been returning any of my calls lately."

"I thought we were taking a break."

"Some break. We haven't been together for four months. Now I don't even get phone calls."

"I've really been busy. You know, with the holidays and all."

"Why the hell don't you just tell me what's going on?"

"Nothing's going on."

He got up out of his chair and went over and tried to kiss her but she turned away.

"Things are more—complicated than that," she said.

"Jesus."

"I just came in to say hello. I didn't want a scene."

"Why can't you be honest with me?"

She reached out and touched his cheek. Gently. "Did it ever occur to you that I might be trying to spare your feelings?"

"I don't want them spared. I want the truth."

She drifted over to the mirror and looked without self-consciousness at her beautiful face. "I'm starting to count the wrinkles."

"You're beautiful. You know that."

"We're not young anymore, do you ever think about that?"

"Sometimes."

"It's going so fast."

"Very fast."

"I wish there were somewhere I could go. Hide out. You know?"

"I know."

"I've started thinking of time as this kind of shambling figure, like a hobo. Sometimes I look out my front window and I imagine I see him there, waiting. I'd like to hide, as I say, but I don't know where I'd go."

"'I have an appointment in Samarra.'"

"What?"

"John O'Hara lifted that from Somerset Maugham, who lifted it from Arabian literature. A man leaves a town fleeing from Death. On his way to Samarra he sees Death on the road and asks whom he's going to see, and Death says, 'I have an appointment in Samarra.'"

"God."

"Right." Then: "I've missed you. I've missed you a lot, Jane."

"Well, I've missed you, too."

"Somehow I don't think we're talking about the same thing."

"Oh, please, Tobin. I really did just stop in to see how things were going."

"You know how they're going. Richard and I probably aren't going to be partners anymore."

"I know."

Tobin went over and leaned against the dressing table. "So you're not going to tell me?"

"Tobin, please, I—"

"You owe it to me."

She said nothing. She looked at her beautiful hands and then at her beautiful face in the mirror again. "I've started thinking about reincarnation a lot lately."

"Last year it was transcendental meditation."

"I think studying reincarnation has been more helpful for me."

"Good."

"You don't need to be sarcastic. Just because you don't believe in anything."

"I believe in lovers telling each other the truth."

"Tobin—"

"I knew something was wrong when you wanted to take a 'break.' But now that I don't get phone calls—"

"Now isn't the time."

"To tell me the truth?"

"It's very complicated."

"Your favorite word."

"What?"

"Whenever you don't want to be honest about something, you say it's complicated."

"This conversation isn't a lot of fun. I think I'd better be leaving."

"It shouldn't be fun, Jane. It should be truthful."

She glanced down at her hands again. "A lot of people were starting to find out about us, Tobin. It was getting messy. You being his partner and all."

"You could always have left him. We could always have moved in together."

She sighed. "But that's what I mean, Tobin. It's— more complicated than that. I'm sorry."

The phone rang. It was the director. "You can drift out anytime you want," he said.

"All right," Tobin said. He hung up.

"I want to see you again," Tobin said to Jane. "I want to sit down across a good table at a good restaurant and talk. I want you to tell me everything. Everything. Then at least I won't have to wonder what happened. I'll know what happened."

She leaned over and kissed him. "I know it hasn't been much fun for you lately. And I'm sorry."

He pulled her to him and kissed her as he'd been wanting to kiss her for months. He was almost dizzy with the grinding need of his kiss. It was beyond sexual need. It was—he didn't know what else to call it, though he'd called so many things this—love.

Then she pulled gently away from him. "You'd better get ready for the show."

"I want to talk to you. Tomorrow."

"All right. Call me."

"I'm serious about this."

"Fine," she said. "Fine. You're serious about this. Fine."

He tried not to notice that, as she was leaving, she was trembling.

3 6:58 P.M.

Peeps was the only movie-review TV show with a live audience. During the final segment of the show, the audience got to tell the two critics what they thought of their criticism. Sometimes the result resembled a brawl.

One unkind critic had called it "Bowling for Movies," but he was probably just jealous because he didn't get to sit in one of the two chairs arranged in a kind of confrontational position and argue not only with his partner but with an audience filled with film students from various schools in and around New York. If there is a group more insular and arrogant than film students, it is still in the experimental stage and has not been mass-released yet.

Tonight's crowd seemed more aggressive than usual. Frank Emory felt it was a good idea to send one of the show's stars out before the taping to establish an "emotional link," as he liked to call it, with the audience.

Which is what Tobin was trying to do now.

"I'd like you to know that we're going to start including more foreign films, the way you've asked," he told the two hundred young people.

"Yeah, your idea of a foreign film is *Rambo Goes to Japan*." Somebody laughed from the audience. Then the entire audience—no surprise here—laughed.

"No, I mean we're going to cover Fellini's new movie, and even do a tribute to Fritz Lang."

"He's dead!"

"So is Orson Welles," Tobin said. "So what?"

"Why don't you cover what's really happening today?"

"What would that be?" Tobin asked.

"Music videos."

"Right. There's a big audience for criticism of music videos." Here he put on a snide voice. "Which Nazi uniform do you like—the red one or the black one?"

"Fuck yourself! You're an old man!"

With that, they began chanting, "You're an old man!" and stamping their feet and doing catcalls with chilling perfection.

Tobin had to go right on pretending to be put out but he knew it was what gave the show its edge and,

18

consequently, its audience. *Peeps* was kind of a pseudo-intellectual version of mud-wrestling, and for the past four years people had been eating it up.

Tobin raised his hands high and bowed, as if supplicating himself to the loonies in the audience, then ran offstage like a lounge singer after his last number.

Backstage he ran right into Richard Dunphy.

Several people around them stopped doing what they were doing and began watching intently.

It was the virtual equivalent of two top guns in the Old West facing off in the middle of Main Street.

Here stood five-five (he used to add "and a half," but that got too embarrassing) Tobin and there stood six-foot-two Richard Dunphy.

Neither spoke a word.

They just looked at each other.

Dunphy said finally, "Hello, Tobin."

"Hi."

"I suppose you remember last night." Dunphy's face shook with what seemed equal parts of anger and fear. "You weren't that drunk." Dunphy was going slightly fleshy but he still had a face that appealed to women in a bookish way. The horn-rimmed glasses and the tweed jackets with the leather patches and the absent-minded air helped. Dunphy always gave the impression he was thinking of something that would have startled Plutarch. Even when he was reviewing a teen-age slasher movie.

"No, I wasn't that drunk."

They fell into their silences again.

More people came. Stood close by. Watched.

Dunphy said, "You owe me an apology. I hope you know that."

"You know what I say to that?"

"What?"

"Fuck yourself."

And with that, Tobin stomped back to his dressing room.

4 **7:02 P.M.**

"There you are," Michael Dailey said as Tobin put his hands on the doorknob of the upstairs dressing room.

He recognized Dailey's voice instantly. Tobin turned to face the man the way you might turn to face a firing squad.

Michael Dailey had made a minor art form out of lounge lizardry. With his slicked-down dark hair, his pencil-line mustache, his heavily lidded eyes, his full ironic mouth, he resembled a gigolo from a thirties movie. He was at least fifty years old. Tonight he wore a narrow-collared black jacket, a brilliantly white shirt, and a red bow tie. It was to his credit that he didn't look silly. Indeed, he looked quite seriously decadent. He was Richard Dunphy's agent.

Dailey extended a hand that Tobin shook reluctantly. "Isn't it time you two made up?"

"No," Tobin said and turned back to opening the door.

"He's a better friend of yours than you might think," Dailey said. "You really hurt his feelings."

"I don't believe it."

"I saw Jane leaving your dressing room," Dailey said.

"I should have expected she'd run straight to you."

The back of Tobin's neck felt tingly. Did Dailey know about the affair he'd been having with Jane Dunphy?

Dailey said, "She should have come to Joan, if anybody. Joan could have helped her and not made the situation worse by stirring up your feelings about Richard again." Joan was Dailey's wife, a former runway model, blond, pale, inexorably of the night. Mrs. Dracula.

"Yeah, right; Joan's the first one I'd turn to in a crisis."

Dailey bristled. "Are you disparaging my wife?"

Tobin sighed. "Michael, what the fuck are you doing up here talking to me? You should be down talking to Richard. I just treated him like shit. He probably needs comforting. You know Richard."

"I'm trying to settle your childish dispute once and for all."

"You're doing a rotten job of it. Anyway, you don't have to worry about Richard and me anymore. Since he won't sign the contract, there's no reason we'll have to be together under any circumstances."

"But that's one of the things I came up here to tell you."

Tobin's heart speeded up. "You mean he's considering signing?"

"Possibly."

But Tobin could see that Dailey was only doing one of his agent routines. "He hasn't reconsidered, has he?"

Dailey was very good. Without in the least admitting that he'd just told a lie, he said, "I think he'd be so overwhelmed by an apology from you that he'd get swept up and sign the papers without thinking."

21

Dailey had just finished his sentence when a young woman in her mid-twenties appeared at the top of the stairs, looked around, then came over to the men.

Sarah Nichols was a Ph.D. candidate who was also Richard Dunphy's assistant, which translated into latest hump. She was a natural beauty with auburn hair that sparkled and cheeks that shone and teeth that gleamed. She was given to cardigan sweaters that took not a whit away from her wonderful breasts and long peasant skirts that thankfully hid nothing of her precious ankles. She had hazel eyes you could dote on for hours. She loathed Tobin.

"I need to see you, Michael," she said. She made sure that her eyes never lighted on Tobin. He could have taken out his little dick and waved it at her, she would have favored him with nary a glance. "Downstairs," she said to Dailey.

"Is something wrong?" Dailey asked.

"Everything's fine. We just need to talk."

"Hello, Sarah," Tobin said as he usually did, mocking the fact that she would not lay eyes on him.

She slipped her arm through Michael's. "Hurry."

"Think over what I said," Dailey called to Tobin as Sarah led him away.

5 7:45 P.M.

When the house lights went down for the first part of the show, Tobin experienced his usual moment of fear. Sometimes he even had a special dream about

22

this particular part of the show: Here sat the two of them, Tobin and Dunphy, America's favorite movie critics, being examined by Martians. Or Venusians. Or some-the-fuck-body like that. Because, see, when the house lights go down and the audience vanishes into the darkness, what happens is these rodentlike beings from outer space sneak in on kind of a sociological tour, to see why two grown men would sit facing each other in the darkness except for a cone of sterile white light encircling them, arguing vehemently about some colored images flashed on an otherwise blank white screen to their right.

But then the APPLAUSE sign came on and the film students did their part by smacking hands together and thus the show began.

Tobin leaned forward, stared into the beady red eye of camera 3, and said, "Whatever you've heard to the contrary, folks, we really do hate each other and we're here tonight to prove it."

Dunphy said, "That's a really brilliant opening line. Really brilliant."

That's how it started.

How it finished was this: Although they had earlier agreed on the Sylvester Stallone movie ("Even by his Neanderthal standards, this is a low point in his mediocre career," Dunphy said) and split only mildly on the new Alan Alda ("All that's left for Alan to do is ascend into heaven and sit at the right hand of God," Tobin said, laughing, speaking of Alda's role as Albert Schweitzer), it was the third movie that gave them the opportunity to do what they wanted to do—find a film they could disagree about bitterly.

It was a "small" movie about a farm kid's first leave as a sailor in New York City. In the course of it he encountered every possible kind of street person—

from panhandlers to evangelists, from rough trade to rude shoppers—and about the impact it had on him.

Dunphy said, "You know, this is the kind of movie that just doesn't come along often enough. It's low-key, it has no pretensions about itself, it genuinely speaks to the heart of each and every American—and it accomplishes all this without a big budget, and without any special effects. I say this is the kind of movie that would make D. W. Griffith proud he was a motion-picture pioneer."

Tobin shook his head. "Since this is a family show, I can't tell you what *I* think D. W. Griffith would have done—but I can tell you what I did. Fell asleep."

Dunphy said, "You sure that was the movie or your hangover?"

Tobin said, "Or it might have been from reading your column earlier in the morning."

"Tell him, Tobin!" screamed a film student from the gloom.

Dunphy sighed. "You really didn't like this movie?"

"No," Tobin said, "I didn't."

"Then I'd say your tastes have seriously eroded."

"You never had any taste, Richard!"

Whistles and catcalls came up from the audience.

Tobin was concentrating on these, which explained why he didn't duck when Dunphy got up and crossed the small space between them and laid a good, if glancing, left hook on Tobin's jaw.

"I owe you this from last night, you little bastard!"

Over the intercom you could hear the director shrieking "Stop tape! Stop tape!" as stagehands rushed to the raised platform where Tobin and Dunphy ordinarily sat.

But they weren't sitting now.

After the punch, and only a bit groggy from it, Tobin tackled the larger man around the waist and hurled him to the floor.

A roller-derby audience couldn't have been more appreciative.

Tobin sat on Dunphy's chest and started pounding his fists into Richard's face.

For his part, Dunphy squirmed and kicked beneath the yoke of Tobin's body, finally bucking high enough to throw Tobin off and into one of the chairs, which promptly fell over.

The audience went even more berserk.

Now it was Dunphy, nose bleeding from several of Tobin's punches, who was on top. He showed Tobin about the same amount of mercy that Tobin had shown him. Eight, nine, ten punches were placed on Tobin's formerly "cute" but now swollen face.

That was when the stagehands descended on them like crazed dogs, pulling them apart.

The audience responded immediately, booing and covering the platform with half-eaten Big Macs, beer cans, Diet Pepsi cans, and even a gooey slice of pizza.

"Let 'em fight!"

But the stagehands paid no attention.

One group held Tobin by the arms and around the waist, while another restrained Dunphy.

"You son of a bitch," Tobin said, "I should have killed you when I had the chance."

Even in his rage he knew it was a stupid thing to say.

Frank Emory jumped on the stage then. He was as white as Joan Dailey usually was, and glistening with his own sweat.

"My God" was all he could say as he looked at the two of them, their faces bloody, their clothes in tatters. "My God."

He really didn't need to say more.

6 8:47 P.M.

Who would have thought that a candy ass like Richard Dunphy would have had the punch he did, Tobin thought as he lay back on the leatherette couch in the cheap upstairs dressing room.

One of the stagehands had gotten him the ice pack that now rode Tobin's face like a hideous rubber growth.

But that wasn't what was troubling Tobin. He'd been in plenty of brawls in his time. They only hurt for the first twenty-four hours; then they were just embarrassing. People got the wrong idea about you. Mistook you for a jerk. Gosh, who could ever think Tobin was a jerk?

No, what was troubling Tobin was the fact that he was thinking about Dunphy. Thinking *fondly* about Dunphy.

In his mind now he saw the two of them back in '64, when they'd first met, as freshmen, at City College. They'd both been attending a showing of Peckinpah's *Ride The High Country,* which some twinky professor who preferred foreign directors was saying good things about but in a twinky professor way. "It's, um, a cut above Roy Rogers, but it's a long way from Antonioni."

Antonioni! That motherfucker couldn't direct traf-

26

fic, let alone good films!

So Tobin, even then a mild-mannered and laid-back type, verbally attacked the professor with the ferocity of an Inquisition cardinal stumbling on a den of sin.

And before he was through, this much taller and quieter-spoken kid he'd seen around the film department a lot jumped in and started verbally pummeling the twinky professor, too, though in a somewhat more respectable manner.

That was how they met and, man, had they been good friends, the best frigging friends in the world, and how did you get from there to here—to wrestling around on the floor in front of a live audience while the videotape was rolling?

He was just about to get up and get himself a drink when the knock came.

He had been deep enough in his memories that the knock had a startling quality, almost the quality of a summons. He raised his head—the beating he'd taken working with his day-long hangover to give him a headache of bitter hunger—and looked at the door.

"Who is it?" he called.

No answer.

Or no verbal answer anyway. But there was a sound. A sound of something falling against the door.

Instantly he knew that something was wrong. Dropping the ice pack on the dressing table, he went to the door and yanked it open.

And Richard fell into his arms.

Tobin got only a glimpse of Richard's face but even that brief look told him of Richard's condition.

By the time he'd dragged the man to the couch, he'd had his first good look at the knife sticking out of Richard's back.

Dagger.

27

Blood.

Jesus.

"Richard, Richard," Tobin began to say. His voice was like a mewl, some primitive human sound that tried uselessly to articulate shock and grief and dread.

"Richard," he said again.

He had him face-down on the couch. Now he was afraid to move him. He crawled down Richard's long body to where his face lay turned up.

"Richard," Tobin said.

Richard had one eye open. Tobin imagined he saw recognition in it.

"Richard," Tobin said. "Who did this to you?"

But when Richard tried to talk, blood bubbled from his mouth and then his eye closed.

Tobin went berserk. "Richard! Goddammit! Listen to me! None of our arguing meant shit to me! We're still good friends! Still good friends, Richard!"

And then he began to shake him, as if life could fill Richard's lungs, and start his heart again, if only Tobin shook him long enough and hard enough.

Finally, Tobin's eyes fell on the common kitchen knife sticking up out of Richard's back.

There was the culprit!

Maybe Richard would start breathing again if only Tobin could pull it out.

So Tobin bent down and put one hand against Richard's back for leverage and wrapped the other hand around the wooden handle of the knife.

He was just pulling it out, his hands covered with blood by now, when Michael Dailey and Sarah Nichols appeared in the doorway.

Sarah Nichols screamed, "My God, Michael! Tobin's killed him!"

7 9:23 P.M.

For all the cops-and-robbers movies he'd reviewed, Tobin had to admit he didn't know much about actual police procedure.

What seemed like dozens of men and women, some in suits, some in white lab smocks, some in uniforms, came and went in his dressing room. Some knelt and did inscrutable things to various pieces of furniture (dusting for prints? looking for pieces of fabric?); some moved among the dozens of onlookers from the show and asked quiet and seemingly routine questions; and some had what appeared to be an arsenal of tools— flashlights, tiny whisk brooms, tape measures.

Tobin watched a great deal of all this backward at his dressing table, where he sat with a water glass half-filled with bourbon Frank Emory had supplied him. He had been told by the detective in charge, a perpetually amused kind of guy named Huggins, to "please wait right here." There had been no mistaking the way he'd meant "please"—as an order.

So now he sat watching as, miraculously, the half-filled glass became one-third, then one-quarter gone. He just sat and stared at it, scarcely conscious he was emptying it. He was trying to figure out how to feel. Or, more precisely, what to feel. In books, shock victims were always said to feel "unreal," in a dreamlike

29

state. Then he sure wasn't in shock because everything was too real, from the puddles of blood surrounding Richard Dunphy's covered body to the tart odors of the various bottles and flasks and vials the police people used in their investigation.

Something made him raise his eyes and then he saw her. Jane Dunphy.

She stood in the doorway, taller than the two uniformed policemen in front of her, gazing inside with a curiously beatific expression. She looked younger, sadder, and more vulnerable than he'd ever seen her, as if she'd cracked completely, then been put painstakingly back together.

Then her eyes raised from the body of her dead husband and fell on Tobin's in the mirror. They stared at each other a moment and then she eased herself past the two cops and came into the room.

When she reached the body, she paused. Then she walked around it as if she'd somehow convinced herself it wasn't there in the first place.

When she reached him, she put a hand on his shoulder and startled him by laughing. "My God, Tobin, this isn't a joke or something, is it?"

He looked at her carefully. "No. No, it isn't a joke."

"He's dead?"

"I'm afraid he is."

"My God."

"Maybe you'd better go over there and sit down."

"I don't know what to say."

"Right now there's nothing *to* say."

Now that he saw her tears, the reality of the moment seized him.

He started to take her hand, and then instantly realized that—no, that was the worst thing he could do.

An image of Sarah Nichols screaming "My God, Tobin's killed him!" cut through his confusion.

A good policeman—hell, the dumbest policeman in the world—would get suspicious if he saw a suspect holding the hand of the deceased's widow.

He stopped himself.

She said, in control of herself now, "I need to ask a question."

"What?"

"Did you do it?"

"My God," he said. "Are you serious?"

He searched her face for an unlikely hint of humor but of course there was none.

She *was* serious. Quite serious.

"No," he said. "No I didn't kill him."

He watched as relief brightened her eyes. "Oh, thank God, Tobin. Thank God."

Then she did the very last thing he wanted her to do in this circumstance: She bent over and took his face in her lovely hands and kissed him. Not on the mouth, true, but gently, gently, a familiar kiss and not in any way a casual kiss.

Which was just when Detective Huggins appeared, as if by magic, and stood by them.

He was there watching as Jane took her warm, teary face from Tobin's. Watching carefully.

"You told me, Mrs. Dunphy, that you and Tobin here were old friends. I guess I just didn't know how friendly."

An eavesdropping uniformed cop smiled to himself. Apparently part of Huggins's act was to provide snappy patter to keep the interrogations from getting dull.

Jane did just what Huggins wanted her to do. Got flustered. "We're friends—good friends—we've known each other since college—we—"

Huggins held up a hand. "It's fine. I understand."

He managed to put just the right amount of smirk in his voice. Not enough so you could accuse him of smirking but enough that he annoyed you.

Now he moved closer to Tobin and all of a sudden Tobin knew why he'd disliked the man instantly. Huggins reminded him of Frog Face McGraw, the eighth grade's most notorious bully. In addition to cracking Tobin across the naked ass with a whiplike towel, in addition to sneaking up behind Tobin and shouting so loudly in his ears that Tobin was literally lifted several inches off the ground, in addition to taking his new Schwinn and "hiding" it until he finally got tired of the gag and gave it back, in addition to all the garden-variety bully numbers, Frog Face had specialized in humiliating guys in front of girls. The longer he looked at Huggins, the more resemblance Tobin saw—this was Frog Face twenty-five years later, a chunky if not quite fat body, sleek dark hair (though beginning to thin), a face that managed to be almost fascinating in an ugly way, and an easy laugh for someone else's grief. Now, confirming Tobin's suspicions that he was Frog Face reincarnated, Huggins said, "I thought show-biz people were cutting out all that kissy-face stuff. With all the diseases around."

"It wasn't kissy-face," Jane said, her face exploding into a blush. "We're . . ."

Tobin stood up from his chair. Touched her hand. "He's just trying to rattle us. Don't give him the satisfaction."

"You were about to say something, Mrs. Dunphy. You were about to say, 'We're . . .' I believe you were going to explain your relationship to Tobin here."

"We're friends, that's all I was going to say. We're friends."

"I see." He looked at them and his dark eyes, nearly

as shiny as his hair, became ironic again. "Friends. Yes." Then he said, "There's a lunchroom downstairs, Mr. Tobin. I wonder if you'd meet me down there in ten minutes." He indicated the crowd of police officials in the room. "This isn't a good place to talk."

Tobin waited for a smart remark. When none came, he said, "Ten minutes. All right."

Huggins turned to go and then said, "I know what good friends you are, Mrs. Dunphy, but I'd really like to talk to Tobin alone." He smiled. "You can get back to your personal business later tonight."

She flushed again.

8

10:46 P.M.

"He wasn't going to sign the contract, was he?"

"Apparently not."

"And if he didn't, the show wouldn't be nearly as strong, would it?"

"Maybe it wouldn't have been."

"In fact, Mr. Tobin, without him, there might not have been any show at all, would there?"

"I can't say. It'd be too speculative."

"And that's why you hit him last night, wasn't it?"

"'Hit' him is too strong. I swung at him. Brushed him, more than anything."

"And then again tonight—while your show was taping—even then you couldn't restrain your anger. You got into it again."

"If you got your facts correct, you'd know he started it."

"But you didn't try to stop it. You got down there on the floor and started punching back."

"I was angry."

"Obviously."

"But not angry enough to kill him."

"Let's say I give you the benefit of the doubt."

"Gee, thanks a lot."

"Understand one thing here, Mr. Tobin. I take shit from only two people—my captain and my wife. You don't happen to be either of them."

"All right."

"So let's say I give you the benefit of the doubt. Let's say that last night was a fluke and that tonight was all Dunphy's fault. Let's say you're just a sweet little altar boy wandering around in a world of wolves. Let's say all these things."

"All right. Let's say them."

"There's still one thing that bothers me a great deal."

"What's that?"

"Jane. His wife."

"What about her?"

"What about her? Jesus Christ, are you kidding me, what about her?"

"No, I'm not kidding you."

"The way she was kissing you when I walked up? You've got to be kidding me, Mr. Tobin. You're having an affair with her."

"No. I'm not."

"Of course you are, and I'm going to prove it. You ready for a refill?"

When their cups were full again with strong black coffee, they went back to the table in the lunchroom where they'd been sitting and started talking again.

Studio people—grips, lighting men, a makeup man or two—drifted in and out, and each of them, whether they got soda pop or coffee or a candy bar, each of them did the same thing.

Stared in a certain special way at Tobin.

A way that seemed to say, You're a nice guy, my friend, but your ass is grass.

"So here you are sitting quietly in your dressing room, minding your own business, probably rereading the Constitution or something like that, when there's a knock on your door and gosh darn if it isn't your old buddy Richard Dunphy, who just happens to have a knife sticking out of his back. Put there, of course, by person or persons unknown."

"That's what happened, yes."

But Huggins kept right on talking. "And then, almost as if he's trying to get even with you for taking a swing at him the night before, not to mention having some good times with his wife on the sly—he falls through your door and onto your floor just in time for his protégée—a Miss Sarah Nichols—and his manager to step up and find you kneeling over his dead body."

"That's the way it happened. Yes."

"That's the way it happened? You're sure?"

"I'm sure."

Huggins stirred the sugar in his coffee. He'd used several packets of the stuff. He'd torn so many of the things open, he'd probably managed to build up his biceps in the process. "How many movies a year do you think you see?"

"Pardon me?"

"How many movies a year do you think you see?"

"Couple hundred, probably. Why?"

"Well, think about everything you've just told me in terms of a movie script."

"I don't follow you."

"Say they based a movie on your alibi—that you were just sitting quietly in your dressing room and Dunphy came through the door—would that make a good movie?"

"Life isn't like the movies."

The smirk again. "Apparently not." Some more stirring. Some more looking around the big plastic room with its lumbering armies of vending machines. Some more nods to police people who went in and out getting coffee for themselves. Then he looked back at Tobin. "Yosemite Sam, huh?"

Tobin frowned. "When I was younger, I was a bit wild."

"Three wives?"

"Four."

"You once drove a motorcycle across a midtown-Manhattan bar, right?"

"Right."

"And you once slugged a critic who called a certain actress ugly, right?"

"Yes. We don't have any right to say things like that. It's not her fault she's not beautiful."

"But there didn't seem to be any other way of making your point?"

"Other than slugging him, you mean?"

"Right. Other than slugging him."

"Not at that moment."

He opened some more packets of sugar. It was a goddamn Niagara Falls of white granules. "You ever watch Perry Mason?"

"The ones with Raymond Burr?"

"Right."

"Sure."

"You like them?"

36

"Some of them were very good, in fact. Why?"

"You know how the jury always gasped a little bit every time there was a revelation?"

"Right."

"Well, think of how a jury would gasp when they heard some of the things we've talked about tonight. Driving his motorcycle across a bar—gasp. Punching out a fellow film critic—gasp. Taking a swing at his partner in a downtown bar—gasp." He was good at this stuff, and so of course he saved his best for last. "Having an affair with his partner's wife—gasp."

"I see your point."

"I assumed you would."

"So you're arresting me?"

Huggins shook his head. "It's a funny thing, the way the world works."

"How's that?"

"Say you were a bus driver."

"All right. Say I was a bus driver."

"If you were a bus driver and two eyewitnesses walked in and found you kneeling over a dead man you'd recently had an argument with—you'd be on your way to the lockup right now. But . . ."

"But?"

"But you're not a bus driver. You've got a newspaper column and you've got a TV show. And you've got a lot of friends. So you're not on your way to the lockup, are you?"

"I guess not."

"But that doesn't mean that you won't be real soon now, Mr. Tobin."

"I didn't kill him."

"You took a swing at him last night."

"That doesn't mean I killed him."

"You got into a fight with him on stage tonight."

"I still didn't kill him."

"And you and his wife are having an affair."

"That's just an assumption on your part."

Huggins stood up. He looked at the pink plastic bowl where the sugar packets had been stored. Empty. "You're our boy, Mr. Tobin."

"I'm not. Goddamn, you've got to believe me, I'm not."

Then he saw the smile and he knew instantly what had inspired it and he also knew what Huggins had been wanting all along.

Tobin's tone had just become frantic—pleading— the way it was back in the eighth grade, when Frog Face had hidden his new Schwinn.

Huggins had gotten just what he wanted. He put the bowl down and said, "See you soon, Mr. Tobin."

Then he was gone.

9 11:16 P.M.

He tried Neely's apartment; he tried Neely's office; he tried Neely's latest girlfriend; he tried Neely's most recent ex-girlfriend. Then he ran out of quarters and had to go into a coffee shop where a young couple in a booth, cheery with impending Christmas, pointed to him and whispered and smiled and kind of nodded—yes, it actually was Tobin of TV fame right here in the coffee shop with them, probably here to do something very human like wolf down a burger or use the men's room.

He got some more quarters and headed outside, grateful for the way the near-zero temperature slapped him around and got him out of the funk the cop Huggins had imposed on him. Standing here on the curb, his breath silver against the light of the street lamps, midnight traffic heading toward the bridges and tunnels that take the suburbanites home, he thought again how ridiculous it all was: Dunphy's death (Dunphy, for Christ's sake, dead) and himself a suspect (his father an M.D., his youth spent boying altars and chasing the chastest of Catholic girls)—himself a murder suspect. Bloody fucking Christ. Impossible.

Twenty minutes later he made connections with Neely. Or started to, anyway.

"He said," said his answering service, "that he will be at Diablo's. In Queens."

"Oh, shit."

"I beg your pardon."

"I said, 'Oh, shit,'" he said, and hung up.

Diablo's was a singles bar where guys who still wore walrus mustaches and secretly dreamed of bell bottoms coming back into fashion stood and preened and perched for the attention of women who, alas, really were Those Cosmo Gals—horny, lonely, and desperate as any marooned sailor had ever been.

Confirming all this was the fact that the sound system was blasting 1977's favorite dip-shit song, "You Make Me Feel Like Dancing" when he arrived. (He had always fantasized about punching Leo Sayer in the mouth. Leo was just one of those guys.)

Christmas decorations floated above the layers of cigarette smoke. Given the predilections of the crowd here, he was surprised he didn't see condoms twisted into the shapes of reindeer floating from the ceiling.

He found Neely after elbowing his way through a mob of dancers and then a mob of talkers and finally a mob of gawking businessmen who were inclining their heads to a tired sexpot of a secretary who was shaking herself into what seemed to be a trance. The man she danced with, balding and given to lapels wide enough to use as boat oars, glanced at the gawkers occasionally and gave them a smug little smile.

Neely sat in the center of the curving bar, where the barman usually stood, as forlorn as somebody in a late F. Scott Fitzgerald story wiping up gin and tears.

"Hey, Tobin. *Qué pasa*, man?"

Tobin couldn't control himself. "*Qué pasa?* Do you have any idea how dated that particular cliché is?"

But then a Cher record came on the system and Tobin realized it was hopeless. In a time-warp bar like this (you still heard the word "meaningful" a lot here), there was no sense bitching about anything being dated. That's why they came here.

At one time Neely had been the handsomest man of Tobin's acquaintance, and that included all the movie stars Tobin interviewed. But now Neely's hair was graying and a gut hung over his belt. He had the look of a satyr gone to sad seed. "You see that babe on the floor?"

"The one thrashing around?"

"Yeah. Her." He grinned. "How about those knock-olas?"

"I take it you haven't heard the news."

Neely's brow knitted. "She diseased?"

"No, asshole, the news about Dunphy."

"Oh, Dunphy, that jack-off."

"He's dead."

"Dead? You're shitting me."

"Right, Neely. I came all the way over to this despicable fucking dive so I could shit you. Sit at the bar all night long and shit the hell out of you."

"You kill him?"

"Very funny."

"I'm serious."

"You're serious? Jesus, Neely, do you realize you're accusing me of murder?"

"Hell, man, you hated him and everybody knew it."

"I didn't 'hate' him."

"Intensely disliked him then."

"We have to talk."

"No shit."

"But not here."

Neely, who could see the dance floor from here, raised his eyes from the dance-contest secretary and said, "Hell, let's just sit here and enjoy the view."

"No way. This is serious."

He watched the secretary. "I can be serious here."

Tobin frowned. "This is where it ends," he said.

"What ends?"

"It doesn't matter."

"Hell, no, man, speak your mind. We're *simpático.*"

"*Simpático.* Right."

"So what did you want to say?"

What he wanted to say, of course, was how could *any* generation that had had such fine and noble ideas as world peace and feeding the hungry end up here— grinding out sex as lonely as masturbation and affairs as doomed as the prayers of TV ministers. And he knew he was no better than the rest of them: four wives, countless girlfriends, two children he didn't see often enough, greed and envy and spitefulness enough for six people.

Now what was apparently the only current record in Diablo's collection came on. Julio Iglesias.

"Neely, please. You're my lawyer. I need to talk to you."

Neely, ruined on his rum for the night, said, "You sure you wanna talk to me?"

"Yeah."

"I'm not the best. You know that."

"You worked in the DA's office. You understand the process."

"A lot of people understand the process. Doesn't mean they can do shit about it."

"Neely, please."

Neely laughed then. "Actually, I should be flattered. You're the first client who's come to me in a long time."

"Let's go to Walley's."

"Boy, that sounds like fun."

Tobin looked around. "At least they don't play Neil Diamond records."

"Hey, man, Neil's cool."

"Right, Neely. Neil's cool. Jesus."

So they went to Walley's, a sit-down place with live waitresses and everything. Neely made a Semi-drunken pig of himself trying to eat his burger (the meat kept sliding out of the bun and the ketchup and the mustard got smeared all over his mouth and hands and all over the table, mostly thanks to the fact that Neely always had them pile lots of extra vegetables on the burger so that absolutely nobody could manipulate such a monstrosity), and he replied to every third sentence of Tobin's by saying "Wow, that's a pisser," or "What a downer."

So after Tobin got all through running down the past twenty-four hours—how he'd taken a poke at Dunphy last night; wrestled around on the studio floor tonight; been seen being kissed by Jane Dunphy—what did Neely say? "Now that's a bummer."

42

"Yeah. At least."

"I heard of this Huggins guy. A real bad ass. Law-and-order type with some kind of vague political aspirations."

"He reminds me of Frog Face McGraw."

"That a boxer?"

"No, an eighth-grade bully."

Neely tried his hamburger again but without any appreciable success. "That's the problem with having them put on extra vegetables. Shit gets all over."

"So I noticed."

Neely wiped his mouth with the back of his hand.

Tobin said, "I'd like to introduce you to napkins," and handed him one. "They're just on the market this month but they're probably going to prove very popular."

"So I'm a slob."·

"You weren't years ago. Back when we were in college."

"It mattered then."

"What mattered?"

"Everything—living, I guess."

"Living doesn't matter now?"

"Not really. It'd all be easier if the world would just end tomorrow—then all the injustice and all the bullshit would be taken care of. Purification."

Tobin smiled wearily, thinking of a running battle they'd had. "Yeah, but who would buy all the Barbra Streisand records?"

"You still don't like her, huh?"

"Hate her."

"You never did have any taste."

The waitress came with more coffee. She looked at what Neely had done to himself. She looked genuinely disgusted.

When she went away, Tobin said, "Neely, look at me."

"Huh?"

"Look at me. At my eyes."

"What about 'em?"

"I'm scared, Neely. They're really going to try to hang this fucking thing on me."

"Sounds like it."

"So you gotta help me."

Neely put his burger down. "Really, Tobin. I'm trying to help you by saying I wouldn't hire me if I were you."

"You're good. Or you used to be. You won a lot of cases when you were in the DA's office."

Neely shook his head. "You really want me to represent you?"

"Yeah. I want you to get all that 'purification' bullshit out of your head and put on a clean shirt and a clean tie and represent me. All right?"

Neely shrugged. "All right, my friend. Then if you want my advice, the first thing to do is make a list."

"What kind of list?"

"A list of all the people who wanted to kill Dunphy. That's what the cops used to do when I worked in the DA's office. They had more lists than they had brains."

"God, it'd fill a notebook."

"Yeah, in his case I guess it would. Just do a top-ten sorta thing then. You know, like Dick Clark and *American Bandstand.*" His voice went falsetto. "'Oh, look, Frankie Valli's number two!' Like that."

"Should I put Jane down?"

"His wife?"

"Yeah."

"You think she's a possibility?"

Tobin sighed. "Christ, I feel guilty even thinking it."

"Thinking what?"

"Well, tonight, she talked about how they were going to try again. That was earlier—then, later tonight when I saw her I sensed—I don't know how to explain it."

"You still in love with her?"

"God, I don't know how to answer that. I really don't. I just assumed I was for so long—but I'm not sure."

"Then if you're not sure about your feelings it won't be so hard."

"What won't?"

"Putting her on the list." Neely made a broad circling gesture with his finger. The waitress, who looked as if she were pissed off at the universe in general and at Neely and Tobin in particular, came over and said, "Yeah."

"Paper."

"What?"

"May I have a piece of your order pad?"

"That's the only thing I'll give you a piece of."

"Funny material."

She ripped off a sheet of her pad as if she were slicing a knife across his throat.

"She may not be the woman I've been waiting for after all," Neely said as the waitress left, and loudly enough so that she'd be sure to hear him. Then he took from inside his sports jacket a ballpoint pen, clicked it, then turned the sheet over to the blank side and wrote something at the top.

He handed the sheet to Tobin. "There."

Tobin looked at it. "Jesus."

"You're going to need remedial reading, my friend. It doesn't say Jesus, it says Jane."

"The woman I love."

"The woman you-assume-you-love-but-don't-know-for-sure. I think that's how you put it, anyway."

"Then who'll be number two?"

"How the hell do I know? That's where you come in. Sit up all night and by morning you'll have your top ten."

"Jane," he said. "Jane." He sounded as if he'd been hit by a hammer.

Neely was sober enough to drive. They stood at his car in neon-splattered snowbanks, their breath silver, shaking hands. A computer sign across the street in a display window said FOUR SHOPPING DAYS TILL XMAS. (He was enough of a Catholic yet that "Xmas" still grated—you didn't celebrate the birthday of X, you celebrated the birthday of Christ.)

"Maybe by tomorrow the cops will have given up on me and gone after the real killer."

But Neely was no help. "You look too good. Unless somebody a whole hell of a lot better-looking comes along, they're going to concentrate on you."

"Jesus, what do we pay those bastards for, anyway?"

"To find new ways of taking bribes, what else?"

Neely laughed then. "Man, Tobin, you look worse than you did the night you found out your first wife was having an affair with that art instructor."

"Having an affair while she was two months pregnant with our son."

"It's a bitch of a world," Neely said as he turned to be caught up in the shadows outside the neon. "Come on, I'll give you a ride."

"No, it's too far out of your way. There's a cab parked up there."

"You sure?"

"I'm sure. Thanks anyway."

"Okay."

Then Neely left, fading into the gloom until the interior lights of his car went on halfway down the long block.

Then he was gone and Tobin stood there for a time before walking over to the cab, as if he hadn't a clue where to go or what to do with himself.

Which he didn't.

10 Wednesday: 10:35 A.M.

In the days when Tobin had been an entertainment writer for a newspaper over in Jersey, he'd often received invitations to press screenings late, sometimes on the same day that the screenings were being held. Despite the fact that most of the good movie reviewing in the United States is done in the pages of newspapers, studios, courting glitz and glamour, had a decided pecking order. *Time* and *Newsweek* reviewers (the very good Richard Corliss, the erratic David Ansen) could have screenings virtually anytime they wanted them. ("You have a cold today? Don't worry, we'll bring the movie to your condo and set up a theater right in your living room.") So could Ebert and Siskel and certainly anybody from *The New York Times* (including the plucky and undervalued Janet Maslin). But not a mere newspaper reporter from New Jersey. Of course, that all changed when the Tobin-Dunphy (or Dunphy-Tobin, as Dunphy always thought of it) TV show went from local to syndicated. Then, boy, the studios became virtual toadies and started offering to let them see movies far in advance of simple journalists, and in circumstances that Tobin-Dunphy (or Dunphy-Tobin) chose.

This morning Tobin chose to go to the Broadway

screening room in the Brill Building. In Manhattan there were several major screening rooms, including the Magno-Penthouse and the Times Square Theater, but Broadway was probably the most plush, with ashtrays at every seat, and an anxious young lady in an elegant gray business suit walking up and down the aisles offering everything except what the eleven men in the seats really wanted.

The movie had been playing for half an hour. It was a big one, too, with Robert Redford and Dustin Hoffman (talk about billing problems) reteamed, this time as a team of private investigators who eventually tumble to the fact that the President of the United States has a daughter who is heavily involved in drug trafficking. Redford was a legendary bore, both on- and off-screen, and Hoffman was a legendary asshole, especially off-screen, so Tobin had to check his prejudices as best he could and simply watch the movie, see if it intrigued him, moved him, made him laugh. But it didn't because in reteaming these two, the money men had failed to add the key ingredient—a script by William Goldman. The movie obviously wanted to recall *All the President's Men,* but without Goldman's funny-tense dialogue, it failed.

So Tobin sat and watched and tried hard to concentrate because he knew he was considered a Redford-Hoffman hater and he wanted to surprise his viewers by actually liking something these creeps did, but he couldn't. They were, as usual, dull. (Tobin had earned an unfair reputation as "negative.") Actually (and he could prove it) 94 percent of all his reviews were positive, and whenever possible he sneaked in reminders of how underused many of our best actors were, from Albert Brooks to Jeff Bridges, from Marsha Mason (goddamn but she was good) to Carol

48

Kane. He liked most actors and actresses and was a big admirer of many adventure films, including the early ones (especially) of Chuck Norris. So he wanted to like this movie, he really did, but it just wasn't a movie he could go for.

He let his mind drift and of course it drifted back to the murder and he saw bloody Dunphy falling into his arms and saw smirking Huggins all but accuse him of murder and saw the sad satyr Neely waving good-bye and saying "It's a bitch of a world." And then he saw himself in bed last night—beyond the magic even of valium—wanting to call his eighteen-year-old son but knowing he was only being selfish, and so for once he didn't inflict his needs on others, just lay there and thought of Jane and how he'd loved her in his sad and clinging way all those years. . . . But did he love her now?

A penlight went on two rows down. Then to his left another. Penlights were like fireflies in the shadows of the screening room. Ordinarily he hated them—too distracting—preferring to scribble his own notes in the darkness. He could read one out of maybe three lines afterward, but enough to finish his review. Then the penlights went off again—as if some secret signals had been exchanged—and so he drifted back to thinking about the murder again and the list he planned to compile today. . . .

Afterward in the lobby, several of the critics had cigarettes and exchanged quick opinions about the film. One liked it a lot, most seemed indifferent to it. Studio people tried to hover discreetly at the edges of the dialogue but you could see them leaning, leaning in hopes of hearing better.

Chamales, from *Manhattan East,* was the first one to bring up what they all wanted to talk about.

"Sorry about Dunphy," he said.

"Thanks."

Robert Chamales was a huge man who always dressed in worsted vested suits—Orson Welles as corporate executive. Tobin admired his writing and liked him personally, except for the old-fashioned English Oval cigarettes he smoked, which invaded the air like green apple farts. "Know what's going to happen to the show yet?"

"Not really."

"Poor Frank Emory."

Tobin nodded. Chamales and Frank had gone to Yale together. Chamales said, "Your show was the only property he had."

"Maybe we can find me a new partner—after a decent time, of course."

As he was speaking, Tobin realized two things: his own crassness (talking about a new partner without expressing any sympathy whatsoever for the fact that his old partner had just been murdered) and that Chamales was proposing himself as Tobin's new partner.

"Why don't the three of us have lunch sometime soon?" Chamales said.

"Sure," Tobin said.

"Why don't I call Frank to set something up?"

"Fine." He was almost stunned by how indifferent they both were to Dunphy's death.

Chamales took out a little leather notebook and wrote out a few lines with a tiny golden pen made even more delicate by his sausage fingers. "There. Fine," he said, dotting one of his *i*'s the fussy-precise way Oliver Hardy would have. Then he said, "I don't suppose you're going to be taking over his screenwriting class, are you?"

"I don't think so." Actually, Tobin had forgotten all

about the class that Dunphy taught two nights a week at City College.

"I suppose he would have given it up anyway. After the sale, I mean."

"Sale?"

Chamales glanced at him curiously. "You mean you didn't know?"

"Know what?"

"That he'd sold a screenplay to Paramount?"

"No. No, I didn't."

"Well, he did, and just yesterday afternoon." He frowned. "Maybe he just hadn't had time to tell you. I heard about it at the Regency. From his agent. Nearly six hundred thousand and half of it up front." The bar in the Regency Hotel was one of Chamales's favorite places. Chamales had once told him that if you sat in there three hours a day and stayed reasonably sober, you could learn half the things that mattered in the entire universe.

"No, I hadn't heard about it." Tobin heard his voice shaking, his cheeks flush. So Dunphy had won the contest. There had been an unspoken competition between them that one of them would someday sell a screenplay and therefore become, without question, the dominant member of the duo. Which is just what Dunphy had done. It was pretty damn unbecoming to be jealous of a dead man, but that's just what Tobin was.

Jealous.

Of a frigging dead man.

He said good-bye to Chamales and went down into the elevator and into a world that was noisy with jingle bells and the sound of the cash register ringing. When a Salvation Army Santa Claus called after him for being such a cheapskate, Tobin flipped him the bird.

11 1:27 P.M.

Tobin cabbed to Hunter College and got out on the east side of Sixty-eighth Street. The sun had appeared. Though classes were out for the holidays, there were several coeds with pink winter cheeks and sparkling eyes of recognition (otherwise eminently sane people went absolutely crazy when you were a TV star and wanted to do all sorts of things for and to you).

He got out of the cab with the list Neely had started for him last night stuck between his gloved fingers. Though he had debated several additional names, he had not come up with any firm suspicions, so he couldn't yet write their names down. He was looking for motives.

Hunter had once invited Nicholas Ray to speak in the sad last days of the director's life, which was how Tobin recalled where the film department was.

A girl in a ponytail and with a breathtaking little ass was standing up at a moviola when he walked in.

"Hi," he said.

She turned around. She had an almost unnervingly sweet face, cowy brown eyes and ripe lips, but when recognition came she frowned. Most definitely frowned. As if she'd just spotted Hitler's son. "You're Tobin, the TV guy, aren't you?"

"Yeah. Guess I am."

"I really resented all the shit you said about John Hughes a couple weeks ago."

"Don't people say 'Hi' around here before they attack someone?"

"It was really bullshit. He's great. Really. Great. Especially *Ferris Bueller's Day Off*."

He was running on caffeine and fear, and so he was ready to go off. The girl's snottiness set him off. "He's just what I said he is. A racist homophobic candy ass."

He could hear the high killer edge of drinking nights and simple animal rage in his voice. This was how he was when he pulled his motorcycle up five flights of stairs to a party or pushed a dishwasher downstairs.

"Some of the staff were placing bets that you killed Richard and I was saying no but now I'm not so sure."

The man who spoke was at least six feet five and he wore a blue cardigan sweater and neatly pressed chinos in such a way that he looked like a private-school boy even though his gray hair and stern, arrogant features marked him as middle-aged. He stank of books.

He came out of an office in which a poster of Gloria Swanson as the Hollywood Medusa in *Sunset Boulevard* was prominently displayed.

"I'm Baines. One of the film instructors here." He put out a lean hand, which Tobin accepted. Baines had a grasp like a snakebite—quick and stinging. "Sorry Marcie was so belligerent. But I guess you're not exactly a wonderful guy, are you?"

Tobin was on the defensive now. "I don't care much for suburban fascists like Hughes."

Baines smiled. "I'm afraid I'm going to have to change my bet, Mr. Tobin."

Tobin shrugged. "Then you'd lose. I didn't kill him."

"From the *Post*, I get the impression that isn't what the police think."

"You read the *Post*?"

Baines laughed. "I even read Dear Abby."

The girl came up and put out her hand. "My name's Marcie Pierce. I guess I was kind of rude."

Tobin shook. "So was I."

"Man, you really do have a temper. You were really pissed."

"I'm under some strain."

"No shit," she said. She looked back at the editing machine and the moviola she'd been working on. A frame of film was frozen there—a ballerina toweling her face after a performance.

"Marcie's doing a ten-minute film on her roomie, who's in dance."

"That's a nice shot," Tobin said. And it was.

"Thanks," Marcie said. "Well, I'm going to go out for some lunch. You want anything, Larry?"

"No, thanks. Already had a bite."

She grinned. "You think I should say, 'Nice to meet you'?"

Tobin smiled back. "Sure. Why not?"

She shrugged. "Well, then, nice to meet you."

When she was gone, Baines said, "She's one of our best students."

Tobin nodded. "Sorry for my temper."

"No harm done." He took a small pipe from his pocket and placed it between his teeth unlit. "Trying to kick cigarettes. This is my teething ring."

"It's not easy. I've tried several times. And failed."

Baines took the pipe from his mouth. "So how can I help you?"

"Well, frankly, I wondered if I could see Richard's office."

"His office?"

"Yes."

"Do you mind if I ask why?"

"I'm not sure why."

Baines seemed to assess him for a long and silent moment during which Tobin became aware of frost on the corners of the windows and boot tracks where snow had melted on the floor. "May I ask you a question?"

"Sure."

"Does this have anything to do with the script?"

"What script?"

"The one he sold."

"No. No, it doesn't."

"I see."

Now it was Tobin's turn to regard the other man at some length. "Why did you ask me that, Dr. Baines?"

"No particular reason."

"You're not telling me the truth."

Baines startled Tobin by smiling and saying "No, Mr. Tobin, I'm not, am I?"

"What's going on here?"

"There was a break-in last night."

"Here?"

"Yes. In Richard's office, as a matter of fact."

"Was anything taken?"

"No one can be certain. But we do know that something was left."

"What's that?"

"This."

From his pocket Baines took what appeared to be a small pin. He handed it to Tobin, who looked at it closely. "It's a union pin. Local 2786."

"Right."

"And you found it in Richard's office?"

Baines nodded.

"And nobody has any idea about its significance?"

Baines shook his head. "Afraid not."

"You called the police, I assume?"

"Yes. Yes, we did."

"Why don't they have this?"

"Well, the fact is, we found it only a few hours ago—Marcie found it, as a matter of fact."

"The police are pretty good at searches. Wonder how they missed this?"

"I consider that curious, too."

"What time were the police here?"

"Around nine. Last night. I'd come in to work on a film I'm making and I found Richard's office forced open and papers strewn all over."

"But Marcie found this pin this morning?"

"Right."

"Mind if I keep this?"

"Mind if I ask why?"

"What if I said I was working on a murder investigation and this might come in handy?"

"They're really moving in on you, aren't they?"

"Yes. That's why I need to find somebody else who'll look good to them."

Baines stroked his face with long fingers. "I suppose I could be a suspect myself."

"Why?"

"I didn't like him and I made no secret of it. I used to do the screenwriting course and then they gave it to him. I resented that. A great deal, actually. I have much better credentials."

"Oh?"

"Sold two screenplays to Roger Corman a few years back, and last year NBC took an option on a mini-series idea of mine. Richard never sold anything except one terrible novel."

Most Roger Corman scripts aren't terrible? Tobin wanted to ask. But a virus of civilization came over

56

him. "Until recently. I'd consider six hundred thousand dollars a pretty decent sale." He felt good about defending Richard. That's what he should be doing, with Richard dead less than twenty-four hours.

"Yes, I'd have to say that was a lot of money."

"But other than yourself, you don't have anybody I could add to my suspect list?" He waved the piece of paper at Baines.

"No, I'm afraid I don't."

"No run-ins with students or faculty members or irate parents?"

"None. He spent very little time here except when he lectured or when he came to see Sarah Nichols." He inclined his head to the open door. "Her office is right down the hall."

"Maybe I'll stop by when I'm finished looking through Richard's office."

Baines smiled again. "I don't recall saying I was going to let you do that. I'm not sure I *can* let you do that. The police have a yellow piece of tape across the doorframe that means *verboten*."

"So you're not going to let me go in there?"

"He may, but I won't."

He didn't need to turn around to find out who stood in the doorway behind him.

"Hello, Sarah," Baines said as she came in the room.

She wore a forest-green sweater that made the auburn highlights of her hair dance in the sunshine. Her discreet brown skirt was meant to be prim but was all the sexier for its good intentions.

She didn't say hello. Just came in and walked up to Tobin and said, "You're not going in there. You have no right."

Her beauty faded a bit close up. She'd obviously spent a sleepless night crying.

"In less than twenty-four hours, you struck Richard twice. Now you're here going through his personal belongings and I won't have it."

Perfect fury blazed in her eyes and Tobin knew better than to say anything at all. He just had to let her work through her rage.

"You knew damn well the public preferred him to you and that's why you wouldn't let him out of his contract—because you knew that, without him, you wouldn't be anything."

He didn't believe that. Not at all. But all he could do was let her yell.

"So you killed him." She started pacing now, and if her gestures—wild hand-flinging and glares that teetered on madness—were somewhat theatrical, he sensed that they were deeply felt, too. He was in the presence of a woman who had loved a man in the most profound way possible, and he couldn't help but be awed and moved by the experience. "You did the only thing you could to save your trivial little career—you killed him. You killed him!"

And that was when she slapped him.

A good hard right hand exactly on the right cheekbone. Enough to daze him momentarily.

His right hand came up automatically, but fortunately he stopped it in time.

She stood in front of him, enraged and exhausted and completely spent yet somehow she found the strength to raise her hand again, but this time Baines took her wrist so she couldn't follow through. He let her fall against him, sobbing. As he led her out the door and back to her office, he nodded silently to Richard's office, giving approval for Tobin to go in and look around.

Which Tobin, a few minutes later, did.

And didn't find a damn thing.

He stood on the corner of Sixty-eighth Street listening to Nat "King" Cole's "Christmas Song" coming from the speaker of a small grocery store nearby and watching people float by with holiday shopping bags and mufflers half hiding their faces. He was waiting for a cab. When one came he got in and gave the driver directions to Emory Communications and that was when he saw them.

Just as the cab was pulling away.

Just when he couldn't do a damn thing about it.

The two of them.

Standing near one of the college buildings. Talking.

Richard Dunphy's agent Michael Dailey and the film student he'd just met, Marcie Pierce.

Dailey was handing her a white envelope of some kind and Marcie was smiling.

Smiling as if she had just been given a Christmas present that included at least half a dozen rubies.

12 5:47 P.M.

"My father's right. I'm not cut out to be a boss."

"Jesus, Frank."

"You want to see the books, Tobin? I mean, would you care to sit down and go over the last P and L? You'd know what a fuck-up I really am."

"There's nothing like self-confidence, Frank." But of course he was lying. He really didn't have much faith in Frank. He'd once attended one of those gaudy conventions where syndicated shows are sold and bartered to local TV stations. Frank had been a Boy Scout in a room filled with child molesters.

"I'm a fuck-up," Frank went on. "I'm not ashamed to admit it. Some men are tall—no offense, Tobin—some men have red hair, and some men are fuck-ups. It's all genetical in the end. All genetical."

"You're drunk."

"You're not doing too bad yourself."

"At least I'm not making up words."

"What words?"

"Genetical. That's not a word."

"Well, it damn well should be."

"Will you for Christ's sake stop pacing?"

"Oh, sure. Sure. Stop pacing so I can sit over there behind the desk. In the boss's chair."

"That's right. In the boss's chair. Where you, as Frank Emory, President of Emory Communications, fucking belong." Tobin waved his sloshing drink as he talked. Sloshing on his sleeve. Sloshing on the couch. Tobin and Emory had been pouring whiskey into empty stomachs for two hours now.

At least he went over, Frank did, and sort of squatted on the edge of the desk. At least he was done with his pacing, which was starting to make Tobin seasick.

"I'm no boss, Tobin."

"Yeah, but you look like one. Six-two. Patrician features. Graying at the temples. Thick wrists."

"Thick wrists? What has that got to do with anything?"

"People admire men with thick wrists. Look at these." Tobin waggled his wrists. "I could be a goddamned fourteen-year-old girl. You've got thick wrists and you should be proud of it."

60

"Three stations canceled this morning, Tobin."

So there went their little run of hysteria. That simple sentence was the equivalent of running down Fifth Avenue stark-naked when the temperature was subzero.

"Three?" Tobin said.

"Probably more. I haven't checked with our sales manager in the past half hour."

"Three," Tobin muttered to himself. "So she was right."

"Who?"

"Sarah Nichols."

"About what?"

"About Richard being the popular one."

"That doesn't have anything to do with it. They're canceling because we're not fielding a team anymore. They like the back and forth. The yin and yang."

"Chamales sort of offered himself this morning."

"Is that the guy who looks like Sebastian Cabot?"

"Yeah."

"Not a prayer."

So Tobin sank bank on the couch and watched the sun set red and purple and yellow behind the frost on the window and let Frank pace awhile and then he said, "I need to ask you a question, Frank."

"What?"

"Where were you about nine last night?"

Frank looked at him and for a moment seemed unable to think. "In the production. Watching the replay of the top of the show and seeing if there was anything we could use before the fight broke out. Why?"

"Just curious."

Then Tobin's real meaning occurred to Emory. "You're asking me if I've got an alibi, aren't you?"

Tobin shrugged. "I guess I kind of am, yes."

"Jesus."

"They're trying to nail me, Frank. I didn't kill Richard, but I need to find out who did."

"God, it wasn't me." He shook his head, dazed. "Hell, now I've got to find a replacement for Richard." He sounded utterly lost. "And if I can't find a good-enough one . . ." Misery gripped his voice.

Tobin stood up, knowing he needed to be out of there, and walked over and slid his arm around Emory and said, "Sorry, Frank. I had to ask. I really did."

Emory smiled bleakly. "I know. I know you did."

"So why don't you go sit behind the desk?"

Emory grinned. "Guess I may as well. Somebody has to."

"That's right," Tobin said softly, "somebody has to."

He waited for a cab in the lobby, planning all the time to go back to his apartment and settle in for the night with a tape of his favorite film, *Out of the Past*. But then, standing there, his fingers touched a round and smooth little button in his pocket. The pin of the damn thing stuck him.

Then, as the Checker pulled up in front, he decided not to go straight home after all.

13 7:58 P.M.
The saxophone player, who was also obviously the star of the six-man group, was as unlikely a Neat Guy as Bill Haley had been in the first place. All

the chunky guy in the lewd red dinner jacket, complete with lewd red cummerbund, needed was a little piggy spit curl to complete the image of Bill Haley reborn. He even had Haley's total lack of talent.

Tobin stood in the back of the union hall (the International Brotherhood of Service People in Bay Ridge), and there in the darkness was reminded of every high-school dance he'd ever attended. The ceiling drooped with streamers, and around a punch bowl wobbled at least two dozen drunks and on the floor short people danced with tall people and fat men danced with skinny ladies and women even danced with women (though this was no homage to Lesbos, simply a tradition necessitated by the fact that some men would rather do anything than dance with their wives), and for every fifty who laughed, ten, inexplicably, sobbed. There was hooch and marijuana on the air and enough Aqua Velva to keep the Green Bay Packers happy for several decades. Across the front of the stage was a big hand-painted sign that read A CHRISTMAS ROMANCE, and beneath it stood the six hack musicians playing cornball rock 'n' roll (which they alternated with slow songs such as "The Great Pretender" by the Platters so, as in the old days, the guys could take their turns dancing with the girls with big charlies) and trying to keep their cummerbunds from falling over the slopes of their guts. But of course the dancers themselves were not exactly Hollywood material either. Holiday booze had given them a certain frantic energy, but there were too many bald pates and toupees and falsies and girdles and shoe lifts to keep them from seeming young and truly spontaneous.

There, in the gloom at the rear of the hall, beneath the ear-thrumming speakers, Tobin felt a kinship with them—grinding out some middle-aged pleasure that, even if it was a tad desperate, imposed some meaning on lives lost in punching time clocks and watching children drift away, knowing that in the end you'd made a fucking botch of it all. Almost as if he were tuned into Tobin's reverie, the saxophone player grabbed hold of Little Richard's "Lucille" and grabbed hold of it good, actually bringing something close to artfulness to his rendition. Tobin, all five feet five of him, found himself alive with music and forgot for a moment about playing detective and allowed himself to be Pied-Pipered toward the bandstand, where the punch bowl loomed in the shadows like a shrine. The guy doing the ladling was as drunk as any of the dancers, and so he got nearly as much on Tobin's sleeve as he did in Tobin's glass, but Tobin didn't give a shit, he just started roaming, still a little buzzy from the bourbon he'd shared with Frank Emory, hoping suddenly that he'd find some unlikely lady here and that together they'd hump through the night (or fifteen-twenty minutes, more realistically, then just sort of hold each other through the night).

He was drifting this way, through knots, clumps, corrals of people, when a hand meant to do him harm began to play trash compactor with his shoulder.

"You think I don't know who you are?"

The guy obviously had a video cassette of *Urban Cowboy* at home and obviously he'd let it have a big impact on him. He was such a squared-away cowpoke that he would have given Hopalong Cassidy an inferiority complex, and he'd accomplished all this without ever leaving the city.

But Tobin knew better than to laugh because even if the guy was a cowboy peacock, the asshole had a hand that could uproot redwoods and a sneer that looked as if it had been put there by a switchblade.

64

"You're here doin' a story on our pension fund, aren't ya?"

"No. Actually."

"Bullshit. I seen you on TV."

"You've seen me on TV, but not as an investigative reporter."

"Fuckin' Reagan wants to bust unions. That's what all this shit is about."

"This may surprise you, but I don't like Reagan either."

"Yeah?"

"Yeah."

"So what're you doin' here?"

"I'm not sure."

The guy grabbed him. He was drunk and he'd been meaning all along to grab him anyway. He had just been looking for some excuse and Tobin had been stupid enough to give him one.

He pulled his fist back and sort of aimed it like a missile and was ready to let go when a guy about Tobin's height but maybe sixty pounds heavier came up and grabbed the cowboy's hand and proceeded to envelop it in a fist that forced the cowboy to let go of Tobin and start doing a whole passel of grimacing.

"You'll always be a fuckhead, won't you, Gilhooley?"

"He's a TV guy," Gilhooley said by way of explanation. He whined. Like a child. Tobin took a great deal of pleasure from the sound.

"'He's a TV guy.' Jesus Christ—of course he's a TV guy. He's a fucking movie critic."

"A movie critic?"

"That's right. A movie critic. Now haul your ass out of here. You understand?"

"Gee, Sal, I was just tryin' to do the right thing."

"Dudley-fucking-Do-Right," the stout man named

Sal said as Gilhooley disappeared into the press of dancers. He put out his hand. "Sal Ramano. I'm vice-president of the union." As they shook hands, he smiled. "And you're Tobin."

"I'm Tobin."

"I guess I've got to say that I don't blame Gilhooley for being surprised at seeing you here."

"I'm just looking for a little information is all."

"Why don't we go to my office and have a drink and see if I can help you."

"That'd be great."

"It's our pin, all right."

Ramano pushed the union button back across his desk to Tobin.

"It was found last night at the scene of a break-in."

Ramano smiled. "I wish I could say that all of our members are good little boys and girls who go to mass twice a day and never say anything worse than 'Fudge.' That doesn't happen to be the case." He flicked ash from his plastic-tipped cigarillo. "Where was the break-in?"

"It was out at Hunter College. In an office in the English department."

"They keep valuable things in English department offices?"

"That's the strange thing—no, they don't."

Ramano leaned back in his tall leather chair and thought a moment. "What you're really asking me is if any of my people are regular B and E artists."

"I guess."

"They're not." There was no hostility in Ramano's voice. He still seemed perplexed by the whole idea of somebody breaking into an English department office. "But I did just remember something."

"What?"

"There's a guy—a few years ago—seems he was taking some kind of night courses."

"At Hunter?"

"For some reason, I think so. Let me check."

Ramano got up and went over to a computer terminal that was covered for the night. He sat down and turned the machine on and worked with surprising speed.

While Ramano worked, Tobin glanced around the office. If anybody was dipping into the pension and welfare funds, he wasn't spending the money on office furniture. This place appeared to have been furnished out of the local Goodwill store. Warped slabs of imitation knotty pine covered the wall; thin maroon carpeting was frazzled in little explosions across the floor; and the desk and filing cabinets looked as if somebody beat on them regularly with hammers.

"Ebsen," Ramano said, scribbling something on a notepad, then standing up.

"Ebsen."

"Harold Ebsen. Used to work in a dry cleaner's when he first joined the union, but then he went part-time last year so he could go back to college part-time and fulfill his dream." Ramano smiled. "Of being a writer. But that isn't what you really remember about somebody like him. What you really remember is how crazy he was. Always getting in fights. Very anti-black, anti-Semitic. Always angry. Just another oddball who doesn't fit in anywhere—but you always sensed he was dangerous. Says here he went back to Hunter."

"You wouldn't have his address, would you?"

Ramano tore a sheet off the notepad and handed it to Tobin. "Here you are."

"Wonder what he's doing?"

"Ebsen?"

"Yeah."

"Well, as I remember, the last time I heard anything about him, he was attending some kind of survivalist classes and writing a book about the coming fascist revolution."

"Can't wait to meet him."

"Take my word for it."

"What?"

"He's nobody to fuck with."

"I'll need to talk to him anyway."

"Then you should go in the daytime."

"Thanks."

"Now I'd better head back to the floor. See how Gilhooley is doing at keeping the peace."

"He inspires a lot of confidence in me as a peace-keeper."

Ramano laughed. "Gilhooley's a lot easier to handle when he thinks he's on the side of the law than when somebody's trying to calm him down."

"Yeah, I can imagine that."

Ramano put out his hand. "I'd go very easy with Ebsen. I've heard very strange rumors about him."

"Such as?"

"Oh, eating only organic foods. Somebody told me he even butchers his own meat."

"You're starting to convince me."

"I'm trying to convince you. Even if you underrate Stallone movies."

"I'm not always right."

Ramano grinned. "So I've noticed."

Then he asked Ramano if he could call a cab, and while he waited in the vestibule outside, he got to hear a medley of Roy Orbison hits.

14

He was headed home again but an image from earlier in the day forced him to rap on the glass separating him from the driver and tell the man he wanted to go instead to Alfredo's on the Park.

Fifty-seventh Street was alive with Christmas decorations swinging in the cold winds. Blue and red and green holiday trees turned in store windows. An angel offering praise to heaven glowed like pure alchemist's gold against a black office building's facade. Even the doorman looked festive, a piece of mistletoe on his lapel.

The man nodded at Tobin and opened the door for him. He had not needed to consult his clipboard. Tobin would of course be invited to tonight's party. That was one of the perks of being semi-famous.

He was shown to the private party room where his first few glimpses were of the New York critical mafia. The occasion tonight was for the Ryder Twins, as they were known, the brother and sister who took a sewing-machine fortune made in Cincinnati and bought their way into Hollywood, where they proceeded to produce, in less than five years, such an amalgam of crap and craft that nobody knew what to make of them. The siblings, Karl and Karla, stood now at the front of the party room. Everybody made the pilgrimage, the way one visited special shrines while touring the Vatican. Karl was cross-eyed and pot-bellied, and no amount of Hollywood cash had been able to do anything about his basset-hound face; Karla looked as if she were trying to be the Baby Boomer's version of Jayne Mansfield. She was given to gold-lamé pedal pushers and push-up bras and actual honest-to-God cigarette holders borrowed from Natasha on the old *Rocky and Bullwinkle Show.*

Tobin spent the first fifteen minutes seeing how much Scotch he could put away and giving a variety of people fleeting cheek kisses (this was the age of AIDS, there was no social dipping) and pumping hands and egos in a way befitting a society bent on having holiday cheer.

There were a few famous people here but mostly it was second-rank because this was a lousy time to pry major-league celebrities away from their families. But of course he was perfectly comfortable, for he was of the second rank too. He saw Chamales, who offered himself again as Dunphy's replacement, and then he answered 1,346 questions about Dunphy's death. And not a single eye that met his failed to contain at least a dim burning diamond of suspicion (murdering your own partner, imagine!). Then he was gone, on to the next set of eyes or breasts or capped teeth. There were orchids in glass bowls and orchids in drinks and orchids on evening gowns. Talk about your festive celebration.

He had come here to see Michael Dailey, Dunphy's agent, but had yet to find him. But in looking he did see somebody who knew Dailey—somebody who shouldn't have been here at all.

Apparently she didn't own a winter cocktail dress because the buff blue gown she wore was summery and reminded Tobin of a prom gown which, given her age, it might well have been. She had her hair done up in a shining chignon and had applied her makeup in such a way that she almost completely camouflaged the fact that she was a film student at Hunter College who got pissed when you insulted a jerk like John Hughes.

So here was one half of the riddle Tobin had come to solve—now all he needed to find was the man who'd stood on the college corner this afternoon and handed her a white envelope filled with what Tobin suspected was bribery money.

But bribery for what? That's what Tobin wanted to discover.

He got himself another Scotch and started over to her.

She stood by a life-size stand-up cutout of the Ryder Twins' latest creation, Gang Girls, two busty ladies in bikinis and low-slung Levi's who made Russ Myers's women look like Betty Crocker. Of course these two had ammo belts slung over shoulders and breasts. Of course they had daggers stuffed inside their spike-laden belts. Of course they held Uzis aimed directly at you. The Gang Girls had thus far starred in three movies with, given the money they made, many more in prospect.

"Relatives of yours?" Tobin said when he reached Marcie Pierce, nodding to the Gang Girls stand-up.

"Funny," she said.

"I wonder if I could ask you a question."

"You can ask. I don't have to answer."

Tobin moved his Scotch from his right hand to his left. "Why don't we shake hands again and see if we can be friends."

"Why should we be friends?"

"Because it's Christmas time."

"Big deal. You don't still believe in Santa Claus, do you?"

He just watched her. "No, but I happen to know that people still give gifts. You got one this afternoon."

Her brown eyes, so lovely, were ruined by suspicion. "What's that supposed to mean?"

"When I was pulling away from campus this afternoon, I saw you standing on a corner talking to Michael Dailey, my partner's agent. He handed you an envelope. A white envelope."

"You're crazy." But when she said it her lower lip trembled.

He touched her arm, feeling sorry for her. All of a sudden she looked like a kid, not at all the hard-edged sophisticate she was trying to be tonight. "You don't want to get involved in any of this, Marcie."

"I don't know what you're talking about."

"Sure you do." He paused. "You probably get financial aid, right?"

"So what?"

"You're probably not from a wealthy family."

"I'm not from a family at all, if it's any of your goddamn business," she snapped. Then her voice softened somewhat. "My father died when I was eight. My mother works in an insurance office. But again—so what?"

"So you need money. That's my only point."

"Most people need money."

"But most people don't get involved in murder cases to get it."

She put her eyes down. He had the feeling she was going to cry. "Just leave me alone."

"I want to help you."

She almost whispered. "Sure you do."

Then her gorgeous brown eyes raised and stared

72

across the room. He turned to see whom she'd recognized. But he should have guessed: Here came her benefactor Michael Dailey. On his arm was the inevitable Joan, looking recently risen from the dead.

"I see you're wearing a blue suit," Dailey said as soon as he reached them. "Don't you think black would have been a little more appropriate, given the fact that Richard just died?"

"Actually, Michael, it probably isn't appropriate that any of us are at this party," Tobin said. "I mean, standing next to a stand-up of Gang Girls and all."

Dailey's cheeks flushed. "This is strictly business. It's the only reason I'm here."

"Right."

"What children you two are," Joan said. "Face it. Richard's dead and life goes on."

Tobin was fascinated by Marcie Pierce's face. The callousness of Joan's remark made Marcie look as if she'd just been told that Elizabeth Taylor was actually a transvestite. The innocence of her shock made Tobin like her all the more.

"You seem to have taken the death pretty hard," Tobin said to Joan. In her strapless white gown, with her hair swept up dramatically and enough makeup on to last a full day under hot lights, she was a plaster goddess. Only her teeth, baby teeth, gave any evidence of real eroticism.

Then she startled him by tearing up. "I don't want to talk about it. It's none of your damn business."

Tobin was about to ask her what was none of his damn business when Michael drew his head back like Christopher Lee eyeing potential necks to bite and said, "We'd best see some of our friends."

Tears remained in Joan's voice. "You seem to forget, Michael. We don't have any friends."

Dailey said, "That's enough of the dramatics, darling. Let's go now." He squeezed her hand hard enough to break bones. You could see her wince under the pressure. Then they were gone, vanished into the land of floating orchids.

"Two of my favorite people," Tobin said to the Daileys' backs as they left.

Marcie looked revolted. "This is a long way from D. W. Griffith."

"Huh?"

"Film is supposed to be about artistic expression. Neither of them have the dimmest idea what art is. They're vultures. And you—" Her grave brown eyes fumed. "You're just as bad—you're a critic."

"I guess I don't necessarily consider that an insult."

"Meaning what?"

"Meaning I do an honest job trying to direct my audience to good films and stay away from bad ones."

"And getting well paid for it."

"Probably not as much as you think."

But by now she had turned away, as if searching out a companion for the evening.

"How did you get in here?" he asked.

"What?" she said, not facing him.

"How did you get in here?"

"None of your business."

"Michael Dailey got your name put on the list, didn't he?"

Now she turned. "So what if he did?"

He surprised himself by reaching for her arm. She didn't surprise him by jerking her arm away. "Don't touch me."

"Why don't we leave?"

"Are you crazy? Me leave with you?"

"Yes."

74

She smirked. "How do you stay out of rubber rooms?"

"I'm not so bad. I'll buy you dinner."

"You just want to find out, don't you?"

"Yeah. But I'm also attracted to you."

That was the second thing he'd said in the past forty-five seconds she found amusing. "Are you putting the moves on me?"

He shrugged. "I guess, yeah."

"Jesus."

"It's Christmas time. I'm lonely and you're probably lonely too."

"If I'm as attractive as you say, then I doubt I'm very lonely."

"Well, maybe just for tonight you're lonely."

"Well, maybe just for tonight you're full of shit." Then she walked away.

He watched her until she disappeared and then he saw an unlikely couple making their way through the crowd. Frank and Dorothy Emory.

Before Tobin could even say hello, Dorothy said, "Don't look at Frank's crotch."

"All right, Dorothy," Tobin said. "I promise not to look at Frank's crotch."

"He insisted on getting a paper cup of coffee on the way over here," she said.

"Honey, I would've been all right if you hadn't slammed on the brakes."

"If I hadn't slammed on the goddamn brakes, Frank, we'd both be in the hospital. The truck ran a red light."

"Well, anyway, that's how come I've got coffee all over my crotch."

"That is *not* why you've got coffee all over your crotch," Dorothy said. "You've got coffee all over your crotch because you're clumsy and because you wouldn't

75

listen to me about not getting any coffee, especially after you'd had so much to drink."

Frank frowned. "See, Tobin, my fault as usual."

But by now Dorothy was already looking around, bored with Frank's coffee and crotch. "Nice to see you, Tobin," she said airily, and then was gone.

"Never marry the runner-up prom queen in high school."

"That's not a very charitable thing to say about your wife."

"If she'd have won, she wouldn't be such a bitch. But she's never forgiven herself for losing, especially to somebody who was knocked up at the time they were putting the crown on her head."

"The queen was knocked up?"

"Yeah, and by a Puerto Rican, at that."

"Sad tale, Frank."

"You don't like her, do you—Dorothy, I mean?"

"Not much."

"How come?"

"Because you're my friend and because she makes you eat too much shit."

"How much is too much?"

"Anything that doesn't fit into a lunch bag."

"Well, at least she's beautiful."

"She is that." And she was—shining blond, with legs up to here, and an erotic teasing mouth and breasts that seemed to pout at you. As if to disguise all this, she generally dressed in conservative clothes and feigned disapproval of anything even faintly sexual.

"Say, you missed the excitement tonight."

"What?"

"Break-in. At the studio."

"You're kidding."

Frank, still drunk, looked at him earnestly. "No, Tobin; why would I kid you about that?"

"It's just an expression, Frank. Christ."

"Well, anyway," Frank said, kind of wobbling on his heels, "there was a break-in. Dunphy's dressing room."

"God."

"What?"

Tobin told Frank about the break-in at Hunter College. Dunphy's office.

"Shit," Frank said.

"Exactly."

"Wonder what they're looking for."

Tobin, who had been thinking about this occasionally over the past six hours, said, "Did you know Richard sold a movie script?"

"Not until this morning."

"So you weren't aware he was writing one?"

"No. Weren't you?"

"No," Tobin said.

"Well, you know how Richard was. He always liked to surprise you."

"I know. But he also couldn't keep a secret."

"That's true. Now that you mention it."

"All the time he was writing a novel, that was all he talked about. He knew I'd be jealous."

"You were jealous?"

"Sure," Tobin said.

"Why didn't you just write your own?"

Tobin sipped his drink. "Either I'm saving myself for the right time in my life, or I don't have a novel in me."

"So you think he would have said something to you about the screenplay?"

"Right."

"I guess that is kind of weird, now that you mention it."

"More than kind of."

"Oh, damn."

Tobin knew what Frank was frowning about without

asking. Frank's wife was waving him over to meet the Ryder twins. Frank, who had an M.B.A., felt a vague contempt for show-biz people and the Ryder twins were the worst sort of the breed. Being in their company was like spending time with your maiden aunt while all the other kids were outside playing baseball.

"Well," Frank said. He left, shaking his head.

For the next twenty minutes Tobin made the rounds. He discovered that Dunphy's death had made him a sought-after celebrity. Everybody had questions and condolences for him. He ogled breasts, stifled yawns, peed three times (he needed some food), exchanged glares with another set of TV critics (suburban boys they were, overripe and gushy, who seemed to enjoy nothing so much as a bad "campy" science-fiction movie), and found himself staring wistfully at Marcie Pierce, who seemed fetchingly lost, wandering about in her summer prom gown, apparently in search of somebody who wanted to talk about D. W. Griffith.

He was on his way to the john for the fourth time (he was going to have to load up on shrimp when he got back or else his wrist was going to get sore from doing and undoing his zipper) when he saw the slap Joan Dailey gave Peter Larson.

The two had stepped out of the party proper. They didn't see him as Tobin approached so he watched a minute and a half of their arguing. Then the slap.

"You bastard," she said. "You know you owe it to me."

It was then that Larson saw Tobin coming toward them. He shushed her and nodded at Tobin. Joan, beautiful in her brittle way, drew into herself, straightening her shoulders, preparing a social smile.

"Hello, again," she said to Tobin.

"Hi."

"We were just having a little chat. Very noisy in there," Peter Larson said. Larson was a producer who did "serious" middle-brow movies on big themes such as War and Death and Intolerance. A few of them had starred Meryl Streep at her histrionic worst. (Tobin was of the opinion that her appearance in *Sophie's Choice* was one of the great unheralded comic performances of all time—"Thing you berry mooch—" Sophie says; gimme a break, Meryl—second only to Jane Fonda's in *Julia,* when Fonda played the gushy plaster saint Lillian to the whiskey-ad mannequin of Jason Robards's Dash.) In the last two years, Tobin and Dunphy had had particularly virulent arguments over the Larson films. Dunphy, in fact, had been one of the few major critics to give Larson good reviews.

"Why don't we go back in and have another drink, Joan? It's getting a bit chilly out here," Larson said. He was a fleshy man, once quite good-looking, but now he was sliding into sedentary middle age, and his charm seemed to depend on the fact that he could rarely be glimpsed without his tuxedo on. Tobin wondered if he wore tuxedo jammies, too.

"No need to hurry off because of me," Tobin said.

"I don't know what it is about you, Tobin," Joan said, "but every time I see you I want to hurry off."

"Now, now, that's not necessary," Larson said, embarrassed.

"After all the terrible things he's said about your movies."

"Joan, please . . ." Larson said.

"It's all right," Tobin said. "Joan always has been a terrible drunk."

Tobin got out of there before she could get another shot off at him.

When he got back into the party room, he saw that he was just in time for some sort of event. The lights went down. A spotlight erupted across a small raised platform in the front of the room. And then there they

79

were—the Gang Girls themselves, wearing "Xmas" bikinis of the tiniest kind, with pieces of mistletoe dangling from their breasts and their panties, Uzi machine guns cradled in their arms.

Tobin had attended a bullfight once and heard the same spontaneous reaction that deafened him now— there the bullfighter had gotten wounded, here sex was served up in a mock-serious way that made the party-goers slightly crazy.

Within moments, the Ryder twins had joined their creations on stage. "Isn't this what it's all about?" Karl Ryder yelled.

"Living in a land that lets you make beautiful money?" Karla Ryder yelled back.

And everybody went bug-fuck. What were they applauding exactly? Tobin wondered. Free enterprise? "Xmastime"? The outrageousness of Karl and Karla's hokey-dokey flag-waving number? The Gang Girls shook their mistletoe and their Uzis and the crowd applauded. (Christ, there was Stanley Kauffman pounding the hell out of his hands; would he review the girls' breasts for *The New Republic*?)

"Do you have anything to say to this wonderful crowd?" Karla screamed at the girls.

"Just that we LOVE you and want to be your Gang Girls!" shouted the blonde.

"And please you in ANYWAY we can!" shouted the other.

Tobin wondered if this was the longest piece of dialogue either of them had ever had to memorize.

He couldn't take it anymore and so did the only thing he could. Went back into the men's room to beat his kidney against the rock once again.

He had just flushed the urinal and was headed for the sinks when he saw Tom Starrett standing there combing his hair. Starrett got more mileage out of a comb than anybody had since Edd "Kookie" Byrnes. Starrett, tall, "into" bodybuilding, was a Manhattan attorney who represented many show-biz clients, including Richard Dunphy.

When he saw Tobin in the mirror, Starrett frowned. Good hack that he was, Starrett made his client's enemies his own. Dunphy and Tobin had not exactly ended up friends.

He had a mane of hair, Starrett did, blond, and he kept combing all the time he talked, combing and angling his face in the mirror like some dumb male model trying to get the best angle for the camera. He looked like a disco's idea of Adonis.

"He wasn't going to sign with you again," Starrett said. "So you probably did the right thing." He paused dramatically. "Killing him."

"I didn't kill him."

"Right."

"Fuck yourself, Starrett."

He kept combing. "Every one of you bled the poor man. Every one of you." Starrett loved to give courtroom sob stories, apparently even in the men's room. "Frank didn't pay him what he was worth. His wife clung to him even though she knew he didn't love her. And even his own agent stole from him."

The last bit of news surprised Tobin. "Michael Dailey stole from him?"

"Get ready for one of the biggest lawsuits you've ever seen. By the time I get done with that lounge-lizard son of a bitch, Alpo wouldn't buy him."

"You're sure of this?"

"You're goddamn right I'm sure." Then he smiled. "But a lawsuit's nothing compared to what you're going to get."

Finally, he put his comb away. "You're going to get the chair, Tobin. The fucking chair."

"Been watching Cagney movies again, huh, Tommy?"

Starrett was six-two. Tobin five-five. Starrett said, "If you weren't such a little bastard, I'd beat your face in." Then he smiled again. "But I'm just going to let the cops do that."

Then he patted his hair and went back into the party.

Tobin wandered back via the phone booth. He checked in for messages. Nothing urgent except that his daughter, sixteen, needed money. But that did not fall under the heading of new news.

When he got back to the party room, he saw that Marcie Pierce had managed to get herself bombed and was standing in the corner hugging her drink to her wonderful chest as if it were a teddy bear.

He went over and said, "Do you like *In a Lonely Place?*"

She just stared at him. "You're trying to tell me you like Nicholas Ray?"

"Sure I do."

"Then why don't you ever mention him on that shitty show of yours?"

"Ask Frank. He has research that says viewers hate Golden Oldies shows."

"Research. It sucks."

"I agree. But I'm not the boss."

She nodded to Frank. "Well, he won't be boss much longer." She smiled then at Tobin, smiled in a way that chilled his middle-aged soul. "I mean, without Dunphy there, you and Emory are out of a job. Dunphy was the show."

She'd meant it to hurt him, and for some reason he was stupid enough to let it do just that. He stood there as if frozen—feeling at the moment completely isolated from the rest of humanity (no man is an island but some are peninsulas)—and then he couldn't hear anything, as if he were tripping out on some exotic drug (hashish used to do such things to him), and he felt as if he would cry or go machine-gun-berserk, he wasn't quite sure which.

All he knew for sure was that he needed to get away from it all—the bitchiness, the malice, the careering, and the ludicrous Gang Girls who were still offering themselves like big bikinied presents. He missed seeing his children, and thought of his dead father, and worried in a dumbstruck way that he was just as shallow and amoral as he sometimes feared. This was a very dangerous kind of drunkenness and he knew it.

She saw it in his face, Marcie Pierce did, because suddenly the hardness was gone and she looked embarrassed and then sad and started to reach out for him, but this time it was he who shook her hand away.

"Tobin, Jesus, that didn't come out the way I meant it."

"Screw it," he said.

"C'mon, I'm sorry. Really."

"I know you are."

"You being sincere?"

"Yeah."

"I mean it. Oh, fuck it."

"Yeah."

And then he left.

Frank called to him, and then Michael Dailey, and then Marcie Pierce, but he needed to be outside and alone.

He stood in the hard cold of the night. Snow plows like yellow burrowing bugs worked their way up the street while a group of Salvation Army singers flung their voices uselessly into the whipping wind and snow.

He started to cry and actually managed to convince himself he was only tearing up because of the cold.

Then from behind him he heard the sort of whistle you can only get when you put two fingers in your lips and are willing to risk future lung capacity to set world records. All over the city, dogs were probably going crazy.

She was a few feet behind him, doing the whistling. Her coat was flung over her arm and here she was, subzero, wearing a summer cocktail dress. She'd even managed to bring her cocktail along.

"What the hell are you doing?"

"Whistling for a cab."

"Why?"

"Because we need one."

"Why do we need one?"

"Because we're going to your place and I read this article about you one time that said you always took cabs."

"That's because I got drunk once and was picked up for driving under the influence. Fortunately, I didn't hurt anybody. But I handed over my license and haven't been back to pick it up."

"Yeah, I read that, too." She nodded to a Checker kind of fishtailing toward them in the flurries. "Here's the cab."

"You sure you want to do this?"

"Positive."

Tobin and Marcie got in, then the Checker started fishtailing its way up the street again.

Marcie pressed into Tobin with her lovely breasts and whispered to him, "But if you think I'm going to tell you anything about my deal with Michael Dailey, you're fucking nuts."

"Where to?" the cabbie said.

"You want some of this?" Marcie Pierce said, splashing her champagne like golden water across the air of the cab.

15 11:38 P.M.

"Boy, this is nice."

"Thanks."

"You decorate it?"

"No, actually my last girlfriend did."

The ride and the cold and the snow had made Marcie reasonably sober again and now there was an anxious edge in her voice. She was no longer a femme fatale but instead a very young woman in an older man's apartment.

She walked around, glancing up at the skylight, at the wide fieldstone fireplace, at the bay windows that overlooked Fifth Avenue ablaze with Christmas trees and Santa Clauses lit from the inside so their cheeks were bright pink and their eyes a startling blue.

"God," Marcie said. "Wouldn't it be nice to be young again and believe in all that shit?"

Crikers—could you really be that maudlin at her age? he wondered. Then he smiled. Of course you could. He'd been so himself.

"Well, now there are compensations."

"Such as what?"

"I think I appreciate living more the older I get."

Plus he got to see movies. Movies balmed and moved and excited him as nothing else did. It was holy to sit in the darkness of a theater.

She offered him a bruised smile. "I guess I'm not at that age yet."

"You're really unhappy?"

"Yes."

"I'm sorry."

"So am I." Then she saw his cassette library and moved toward it as if a preacher had called her forth. "Wow, how many tapes do you have?"

"Three hundred."

"Do you mind?"

"Not at all. As a matter of fact, I think I'll go wash up."

She rubbed her bare shoulders as if she were freezing. "Do you ever sort of, you know, just sleep with women, I mean without doing anything?"

"Sometimes. Sure."

"If I decided that's all I wanted to do, would that be all right?"

"Of course."

"You wouldn't push it or anything."

"No, I wouldn't."

"Thanks. That makes me feel better."

He smiled. "Maybe even a little bit happy?"

"Yeah. Maybe even a little happy."

He was halfway to the bathroom (he was planning later on removing his liver and taking it downstairs to the laundry room and putting it in the drier) when the living-room phone rang.

Neely, his lawyer, said, "Huggins may call you in for questioning tomorrow."

"How'd you learn that?"

"Since I decided to be your lawyer, I also decided I

better start calling in some favors from my DA office days."

"So I'm still his favorite?"

"Afraid so."

Tobin looked back to Marcie Pierce. Against the built-in bookcases and the jungle of ferns and plants, against the 45-inch TV set, against the sliding-glass library of video cassettes she looked almost frail and girlish. A huge poster of Orson Welles as Citizen Kane gazed down on her, seeming to leer appreciatively at her young flesh. Tobin whispered into the phone, "Neely, I'm really scared."

"It's going to be all right."

"Really?"

A pause. "I'm not one hundred percent positive it's going to be all right. But I'm pretty positive."

"Well, give it to me in percentages."

"What in percentages?"

"If you're not one hundred percent positive things are going to be all right, then what percentage positive are you?"

"Jeeze, Tobin. That's not fair."

"What percentage?"

"Well, at least forty."

"Forty!"

Marcie turned around as if Tobin had thrown something at her.

"Well, fifty then," Neely said.

"That's the best you can do? You're supposed to be reassuring here, Neely, and you're not reassuring me for shit."

"All right, then, let's make it between fifty-five and fifty-eight."

"Fifty-five and fifty-eight?"

"Yeah, I'm between fifty-five and fifty-eight percent

positive that things are going to be just fine." By the end he was gushing with optimism. "Fifty-five to fifty-eight. No doubt about it." Then he paused. "How's your list coming?"

"I added two more names tonight." And he had, too: Michael Dailey, because he had apparently been embezzling from Dunphy, and a man named Harold Ebsen because he may have been the one to break into Dunphy's Hunter office.

"Good boy. Bring them along to Huggins's office. They'll help. And keep your chin up, okay?"

"Yeah. Fifty-five to fifty-eight."

"Exactly, my man, exactly."

"I see you've got Anthony Mann's *The Naked Spur* out there."

"Yes."

"It's one of my favorite movies."

"Mine, too."

"Jimmy Stewart really shocks you, doesn't he? I mean, you don't expect him to even be capable of a performance like that. So crazed and everything."

"We've always underestimated him. We take him for granted too much."

They were in his bed. She'd made him light the tiny Christmas tree on his bureau, and now the room was cast in deep shadows from red and yellow and blue and green lights.

She had let her hair down and wore a pair of his pajamas and was propped up against the back of the bed as if she planned to sit up and talk all night. She'd taken a shower and smelled wonderfully clean. Tobin had one of those punitive hard-ons that he could find nothing to do with, just lie there and sort of try to flick down and be miserable with.

Thus far, in an attempt to show her that he was a nice guy with whom she had a lot in common (in fact, their taste in films was identical), he'd let her talk on about many of the mutual favorites: Budd Boetticher and Douglas Sirk and Bernard Herrmann, the composer, and Francis Ford Coppola and Martin Scorsese and Robert De Niro and *Out of the Past* and *Charley Varrick*.

Then finally he just rolled over and did it, brought her to him and really kissed her. They'd made a pass at it before, but this time it truly happened. She even parted her lips and let his tongue come in and then it was as if he were in the electric chair and she had just dropped the switch.

Fortunately, she seemed to be as much in need of him at that moment as he of her. So she didn't stop him when his hand found her heartbreakingly gorgeous breast, nor when his legs began to entwine with hers.

It was one of those sweet little sessions, very passionate at first but ending up very tender, his head between her legs, almost as if he were praying in a shrine, her hand gently stroking his head (he might have been her child) as he brought her to release, and finally, when he was cradled inside her and just about to come himself, she said, "Thanks for putting up with me tonight, Tobin."

"That's all right," he whispered back. "Thanks for putting up with me. I'm not exactly a prize."

And then he died the death of pure pleasure and lay beside her watching as snowflakes hit the bedroom window and melted and slid down the black glass, and as the Christmas tree's lights alternated flashing colors.

She was asleep in moments, and moments later he was, too.

* * *

He woke up a few hours later subconsciously expecting to find her across the bed from him. But he patted empty space. Cold empty space. Then one eye came open, then another, then he did a half-push-up and looked around the bedroom. Her prom gown was tossed with teenage abandon over the chair. Where had she gone?

When he decided she was in the living room, he assumed she was watching a movie, maybe *The Naked Spur* they'd been discussing.

But instead she was curled up by one of the windows, looking out over the city. Her hair and her pajamas were tousled and she looked very young and very pretty and he found himself moved in some simple way he hadn't been for many years.

"Hi," he said.

"Hi."

"Couldn't sleep, huh?" He found his voice tender, the way it was with his own kids. Or a woman he'd cared about a long time.

"Guess not."

"You okay?"

"Yeah. I guess."

"I'll give you a quarter if you'll turn around and look at me."

Which she did. Sort of grinning. "Sorry. I guess that is kind of rude."

"So what're you thinking about?"

"Honest?"

"Honest."

"I'm thinking about what I'm going to tell you when you ask me why Michael Dailey was handing me an envelope yesterday afternoon."

"I see."

90

"Because you are going to ask me, right?"

"Right."

"So I've got to come up with an answer."

"You could always tell me the truth."

"Then I'd have to give the money back."

"I see."

She read the disappointment in his eyes. "That makes me sound like a real bitch, doesn't it?"

He shrugged, not quite sure what to say.

"The trouble is," she said, "I really like you now. I really do."

"And I like you."

"And the fact is, I don't like Dailey at all. He's really a creep."

She was going to talk herself into telling him the truth. He knew better than to interrupt the process by encouraging it. He simply sat on the edge of a leather recliner and listened to her.

"Do you have any hot chocolate?"

He thought. "Maybe some of that instant stuff."

"That'd be okay."

"Fine. I'll fix some."

"You wouldn't have any marshmallows, would you?"

"I can look."

"Then will you sit on the couch next to me, when you come back, I mean?"

"Sure."

In the kitchen he made instant cocoa in big fancy cups in the microwave and dropped half a dozen pearl-like marshmallows in the cups and carried them back to the living room and sat next to her.

She leaned over and kissed him and then said, "The only thing we need now is some Christmas music. I mean it's so nice here with the little tree and everything. So peaceful."

"You serious?"

"Yeah."

"Could you stand Perry Como?"

"Perry Como? Really?"

"Yeah."

"I used to watch his Christmas specials. I love Perry Como." She smiled. "Just don't tell anybody, okay?"

"Okay."

So he found his Perry Como record, which he kept in a file behind a lot of other albums—he got tired of record snobs going through his albums whenever he had a party and finding the Como and then running around all night showing it to people and laughing—so he put it on and went back to the couch and sat tight against her there in the Christmas-light darkness and they sipped their cocoa and didn't say anything much at all, just sort of touched each other and smelled each other, just sort of listened to Como do wonderful things with "The Christmas Song" and "Silent Night" and songs like that.

She put her head on his shoulder and said, "This reminds me of being with my father."

At first he felt insulted, at least a bit, seeing that the season and her own turmoil had caused her to turn to him as a father substitute, but then he realized that he'd been able to give her something more substantive than he was able to share with many one-night stands. It wasn't just quick forgettable sex; there was real kindness between them, and he loved her for it.

She started to talk about her father, an insurance salesman, and how he'd died of heart disease, and the struggle her mother had had ever since with money and loneliness and, ironically, with her own heart disease.

Then she surprised him by saying, "But I still

shouldn't have taken money from Michael Dailey. I mean, there are people a lot worse off than I am."

"We do what we have to."

"I think he's broken into Dunphy's office."

"Dailey did the break-in?"

"Not *the* break-in. That came later."

"I don't understand."

"There were two break-ins. One earlier. One later."

The Como record ended and he got up to start it again but she said, "No, that music makes me too sentimental about my father. Leave it off while I talk, all right?"

"All right."

He went back and sat next to her again.

"I usually work in the department at night on my film. That's what I was doing last night when I heard this noise down the hall. It was around seven o'clock and pretty dark and I got kind of scared, you know, thinking maybe somebody had broken in, or it was some rapist or something. But I went down the hall anyway, just to check it out, and that's when I found him there."

"Dailey?"

"Right. Dailey."

"What was he doing?"

She grinned. "Making an asshole out of himself, actually. He was bent over in front of Dunphy's door and trying to pick the lock with a credit card. Obviously it was something he'd seen on TV. The trouble was it didn't have the right kind of lock."

"So what happened?"

"I just kind of stood there and watched him. I wanted to see what he did next." She smiled. "Then the security guard came along."

"What did Dailey do?"

"Really panicked. Plus he looked very dorky. He had on this red lamé dinner jacket and this cummerbund and he was running all over the office trying to find someplace to hide when he heard the guard coming."

"He still hadn't seen you?"

"No."

"So the guard came."

"So the guard came, and I—I don't know why I did this—I stepped in his way and said hello. He's sort of a young guy and always vaguely putting the moves on me. So he stood there and talked with me and then he went on without checking out the inner offices."

"So Dailey got away?"

"No, he was hiding under the secretary's desk. I went in and stood above him and told him I knew what was going on and that if he didn't come out I'd call the security guard back.

"So he got up and tried real hard to have some dignity but it wasn't easy."

"I can imagine."

"Then he made me his offer."

"Which was?"

She sighed. "I'm going to sound crass here, aren't I, because I took it and all?"

"I've done a few things I'm ashamed of in my life." He touched her hand. "About six-thousand-seven-hundred-and-eighty-three things, to be exact."

"He asked me if I could help him get into Dunphy's office."

"Could you?"

"As a matter of fact, I knew where the secretary kept her spare keys, in case one of the professors locked himself out."

"So you let him in?"

She sighed. "Yeah. And I'm really sorry I did."

"How long was he in there?"

"About fifteen minutes. I kind of stood sentry, in case the guard came back."

"Did he seem to find anything?"

"He found something. He had several sheets of paper rolled up into a tube when he left."

"But you don't know what they were?"

"No idea."

"He didn't say anything."

"No—oh, except that he didn't have much cash on him."

"That's what this afternoon was all about?"

"Right. He met me on the corner of Sixty-eighth and handed me the money in an envelope."

"How much?"

She sighed again. "Five hundred dollars." Now it was her turn to touch his hand. "But I haven't spent any of it and I'm going to send it back to him."

"Good."

"I shouldn't have done it."

"I don't think you need to say that anymore. Really."

"Will you hold me?"

"Sure."

"I don't want to kiss or anything. Just be held."

"I understand. I get like that a lot myself."

So he held her for a long time and thought about his own daughter and about his ex-wives (two of whom had botched the marriage; two of whom he caused to leave him), and then a pink-and-yellow dawn was at the frosty window.

She was asleep again. He went in and showered and shaved. He had a lot to do. When he came back out she was making coffee. He'd already decided what he was going to do. He had a check in his pocket and he went over to her at the Mr. Coffee and slipped it into her pajama pocket. "This is for you and your mother. For Christmas gifts."

"God, Tobin—"

He kissed her on the cheek. "No arguments. I'll probably talk to you later today, if I get a chance."

"I really am going to send him the money back."

"I know you are." He kissed her, this time on the nose. "And that's why I like you so much."

"Can I sort of hang out here and watch *The Naked Spur* before I go home?"

"Sure."

"I had a great time last night."

He laughed. "You beat me to it. I was just going to say that myself."

16 Thursday 9:17 A.M.

Harold Ebsen lived in a little stucco house too close to Red Hook to make realtors happy. When Tobin got out of the cab, he told the driver to wait and then he stood inhaling air from the golden winter morning. The block of little houses was occasionally dwarfed by Christmas ornaments that managed to look both cheap and endearing at the same time. Ebsen was not apparently the festive sort. The only decoration on his front door was a single tiny piece of holly, as if somebody had gotten Ebsen down on the ground and threatened to break his arm if he didn't put up something that said Christmas. A couple of kids who looked like lumbering spacemen in their snowsuits walked past Tobin and gave him the sort of openly suspicious look-over only four-year-olds are capable of. One kid had red stuff on his mouth. The other kid had brown stuff. The kid with red stuff also had green stuff but not on his mouth, rather running from his nose. "It's that TV guy," one of them said.

"What TV guy?"

"I don't know. Just the TV guy."

"Oh."

Tobin went up the walk that needed shoveling. If the police didn't think he was a murderer, he would have enjoyed himself, sunny winter days being one of the few things that invigorated him these days. The foundation of the house had shifted dramatically to the right. Then he noticed that both windows on either side of the front door were painted black. He hadn't seen that since hippie days. He knocked. Then he knocked again. While he waited he waved to the two kids in snowsuits who were angled out from behind an oak tree watching him and saying things back and forth with breath that shone silver in the daylight. Then he turned around and knocked some more. From the curb he could hear the cab radio playing country/Western (Tobin was a Hank Williams fan; he hated groups like Alabama). He gave the song a few more bars and raised his hand to bring it down on the door once more and then a voice said, "Over here."

Tobin turned to his left and looked over the edge of the porch railing.

A big man with thick rimless eyeglasses and blackheads the size of meteorites stood glaring at him. This had to be, from Ramano's description, Ebsen himself.

Over his fleshy, hairy chest had been tugged a sleeveless T-shirt two or three sizes too small. Draped over his forearm and hand was a shirt of some kind. He pointed the shirt at Tobin and waved the shirt around a little bit and then all of a sudden Tobin realized what the shirt was hiding. His throat got dry and he was tempted to turn around and yell for the cabbie to call the cops, but then he looked again at Ebsen and thought, This bastard is certifiable. Look at those eyes. The long-lost twin of Richard Speck.

"You ain't gonna screw me out of it the way he did," Ebsen said.

"Screw you out of what?"

"Get your ass inside that door."

Tobin nodded. "This door?"

"That door, you asshole."

Tobin looked back at the cabbie and thought about yelling again and then decided against it. He started to put his hand on the door when, peripherally, he saw something like a miracle.

The two snowsuited kids came up the walk.

"You are too the TV guy, aren't you?" said the one with brown stuff on his mouth.

"You ain't neither, are you?" said the one with red and green stuff.

"Yeah. Yeah. I am the TV guy." When he heard his own voice, he realized he could barely talk. His stomach felt bad and his bowels felt worse. He was scared.

"See, I told you, Lonnie."

"Just 'cause he says he is don't *mean* he is."

"You kids get out of here," Ebsen said.

"Hi, Harold, you pissed off or something?" the one with chocolate said. Four years old. And saying "pissed off." Tobin felt outraged, as if he were a PTA member dealing with swearing among tot-lot attendees. (He'd once known a couple—back in the good-bad old days of the sixties—who'd taught their kid to say "fuck," and every time he said it, the worst sort of Catholicism came over Tobin and he wanted to steal the kid and hand him over to the nuns.)

"I said, get outta here."

"All we're doin' is playin'."

"Goddammit, you two. Out." Ebsen moved around the corner of the house fast enough to have the effect on them he wanted—they spooked and ran, back to their hiding place behind the elm tree. Ebsen then came up behind Tobin and jammed the shirt against Tobin's back.

"Now get inside. You hear me?" Ebsen didn't need a gun to be scary. He was maybe six feet five and two hundred and fifty pounds, and he gave the impression that he probably spent at least some of his time tying cats inside gunnysacks and tossing them in the river.

"You sure you know what you're doing?"

"What the fuck's that s'posed to mean?"

"I mean," Tobin said, realizing how naive he sounded, "that just doing what you've done so far— just waving a fucking gun at me—I mean that's five-to-ten in Attica."

"I'm real scared. Don't I sound real scared?"

"I guess when I think about it you don't sound very scared after all."

"Good. Now get inside."

Tobin's eyes went back to the kids again. Why couldn't those dumb little bastards be telepaths and read his mind and then go call the cops?

"Move," Ebsen said.

Tobin put a hand on the door. Swallowed hard. Turned the doorknob. "Five-to-ten. You really better think it over, Harold. Really."

"Inside."

So he went inside. His first impression, with his eyes

tearing up and his stomach starting to churn, was that Harold was running a slaughterhouse out of here.

Most of the living room looked pretty normal if your standard was a late-sixties crash pad whose owner skewed to the right. There was a biker poster featuring a fat guy and a fat woman in their best leathers on a Harley that looked bigger than a Buick. There was a Confederate flag. There was a glassed-in collection of knives, any one of which looked formidable enough to disembowel a three-hundred-pound man. There were guns of every kind imaginable—rifles, handguns, shotguns, something that might have been an Uzi. (There were a lot of Uzis in Charles Bronson pictures, and Tobin had seen three Charles Bronson pictures within the last five months, Charlie understandably cashing in on the waning days of his bankability.) There was furniture, too, of course, the sort that looked as if old Harold here might have grabbed the Uzi and hijacked himself a Salvation Army truck—one headed for the dump. There was a couch, torn and faded red, and a green armchair with what appeared to be three bullet holes in one of the arms (just one of the hazards of modern urban living), and a 21-inch Motorola TV set that had been manufactured the year Tobin learned his mass Latin. The place was dusty as a Pharaoh's tomb and disarrayed as if the bikers on the poster had invited a few hundred of their friends over for a party. But that wasn't what bothered Tobin. Uh-uh. What bothered Tobin was the table he could see through the archway leading into the small dining room.

"Jesus," he said.

But Ebsen didn't seem to notice Tobin's disgust.

"You were working with him on it, weren't you?"

"On what?"

"You know damn well what. Now I want my cut of

it—just like he agreed—and I want it in cash. You understand?"

"I understand that you want it in cash, Harold. I just don't understand what 'it' is."

"You son of a bitch."

"That doesn't exactly explain a lot."

"You crummy fucking bastard."

This time Tobin knew better than to say anything. Harold was one of those guys who should be shot up with elephant guns full of Thorazine every morning. He stood in front of Tobin now shaking from some terrifying psychic rage that his watery blue eyes made all the more frightening. There was spittle dripping from both sides of his mouth and Tobin could see his biceps bulk up to the size of volleyballs. Harold, in his psychosis and dislocation, needed someplace for his fury to light.

Then Tobin heard the squawk and at first he wondered if his fear hadn't begun to make his mind play tricks.

But the squawk came again and then what was unmistakably a chicken waddled out from the dining room. Then the table in there made sense.

"There you are, you bastard," Ebsen said to the chicken. Harold seemed to be pissed off at everybody today, including chickens.

Tobin raised one tiny little finger, as if seeking permission from a nun to go to the bathroom.

"What?" Ebsen snapped.

"That's a chicken, right?"

"No, asshole, it's a Pekingese."

"I just mean it's kind of strange to have a chicken in your house."

"That's why I'm mad at the bastard."

"Why?"

"He's s'posed to be outside with the rest."

"The rest of the chickens?"

"Yeah, the rest of the chickens."

"How come you have chickens?"

"C'mere, you little asshole," Ebsen said. He was on his knees and putting a hand out the way you would for a puppy. The chicken, scruffy and dirty, just stood and eyed him with chickeny contempt. "You're gonna pay, you little motherfucker."

While Ebsen was trying to get the chicken to come close enough to punch out, Tobin of course was starting to look for means of escape. He wasn't sure if Ebsen had locked the door. If not—

"You move, you're dead," Ebsen said. He waggled the Luger at Tobin.

"I'm just standing here. Right here. Plain sight."

"You better."

Then he went back to the chicken and Tobin went back to looking with disgust at the table in the dining room. It was one of those drop-leaf jobs. Both leaves had been dropped and the one in view was streaked with blood. It looked like a sacrificial altar. There were feathers and dried puddles of blood all over the floor.

"You kill your own food, huh?"

"Goddamn right, I do. The shit you eat is poisoned. I buy chickens from this farmer and raise them myself in the backyard. Organic."

"Then you kill them here?"

"Yeah. You mind?"

"You should open a window once in a while."

"You should shut your mouth once in a while."

Then he grabbed the chicken. The move was impressive. One moment Ebsen sat there on his knees talking to Tobin, seemingly paying no attention to what the chicken was doing, and then suddenly his hand shot out and he got the chicken by the neck. The chicken wriggled and wiggled and squawked, and feathers tore away from its body and drifted on the strange air let in by the blacked-out windows. "Little son of a bitch," Ebsen said, standing up again. "I'll teach you to sneak in the house."

"I doubt he did it on purpose," Tobin said, "I mean, he's only a chicken." Tobin knew what was coming and felt sorry for the animal.

"This is the third time he did it," Ebsen said.

"Maybe he just gets cold outside."

"The other chickens don't get cold."

"Maybe he's different from the other chickens."

"That's his problem."

Ebsen put the chicken up on the table and laid him on his side—the chicken didn't have a chance against Ebsen's biceps—and then he picked up an ax.

"I want my money by six tonight, or else I go to the press."

Ebsen was a confusing guy. Here he was supposed to be killing a chicken but he was talking business instead. "And I know he just got a bundle laid on him before you iced him." He looked up through his Mount Palomar glasses. "I followed him around a few days. I know what was going on with those reviews."

"What reviews?"

He stared at Tobin a second and then said, "You really don't know, huh?"

"No."

He grinned. "Then you're a dumber bastard than this chicken here."

Then he let the ax go so hard that the chicken's head flew in through the archway and landed near Tobin's feet. The rest of the chicken, still on the table, jerked in death spasms.

"Too bad you can't stay for some chicken dinner."
Ebsen laughed. "But I'll bet you'd be too much of a
candy ass to eat it. You like to have somebody else kill
your food for you." Then Ebsen put down the hand ax
and picked up the Luger again and pointed it directly
at Tobin. "His wife knows what's going on. You go talk
to her and you tell her if she doesn't want it all over the
newspapers, she better come through with the dough
and I mean today. You understand?"

"I'll talk to her, if that's what you mean. But I still
don't understand."

"Good. Now get the fuck out of here."

"What was the gun for?"

"I wanted to make my point. Everybody thinks that
just because the Army tossed my ass out that I was too
dumb to ever get anything going. Well, your partner
knew better. He knew better real good."

"Got ya."

Tobin was already backpedaling to the door. He
knew one thing—it was going to be a while before he
had a chicken dinner again.

"Six o'clock," Ebsen said.

"Six o'clock."

For effect, just to impress him even a little more,
Ebsen took a hunting knife from inside his belt and, as
Tobin's hand touched the doorknob, Ebsen put the
knife deep into the belly of the chicken and started rip-
ping downward. "Sure you don't want to stick around?
This is the best part."

Outside in the golden morning, taking in golden air,
the two kids in snowsuits came up. "Is Harold still
pissed off?" the green-nosed one said.

"Yeah," Tobin said, getting into his cab, "I think it's
safe to say that Harold's still pissed off."

They shook their heads at each other, then tottered
off.

17 11:47 A.M.

There was a screening in the Brill Building at one o'clock, so Tobin decided, in the meantime, to call on Michael Dailey, whose office was only a few blocks away from the Brill.

A decorator from the low-profile school had done Dailey's office. Despite his flamboyant personal style, Dailey was otherwise one of those men who went out of their way to impress clients with their conservatism. He drove a gray Mercedes. He always kept a copy of *The Wall Street Journal* (instead of *Variety* or *Hollywood Reporter*) on his desk. He lived in a Tudor-style house. And his office was such a discreet blend of earth tones it had an effect equivalent to popping a few Valiums. The only striking thing in the expensive but bland office was a Chagall print.

"Yes?" The receptionist wore—what else?—brown. She was one of those prim middle-aged women whose mouths give just a teasing hint of eroticism but nothing you could prove in court. Then she recognized him, her earth-tone eyes showing a hint of anger. "Oh, I'm sorry, I didn't recognize you at first." Her tone had changed now she had recognized him—Benito Mussolini's brother.

"I'd like to see Michael."

"I'm not sure that's possible."

"Oh, it's possible all right."

"I beg your pardon?"

"I say it's possible because if he's anywhere in the office, then I'm going to find him." His angry edge surprised even himself. It happened this way sometimes. He'd be standing talking to somebody who irritated him and then he'd just lose it. Really start to get nasty. "Yosemite Sam" was back in action.

"I see."

"Apparently you don't see because you're not getting him on the intercom."

"He's talking to the Coast."

"Is the Coast talking back?"

She said, "There was a Detective Huggins here earlier this morning. He gave the impression that you're going to be arrested."

"That would probably make you pretty unhappy, wouldn't it?"

She smiled. "Oh yes, extremely unhappy."

He sighed. "I don't mean to take this out on you."

"Very noble."

"I just want to see Michael."

"I told you he's talking to the Coast."

"Fuck the Coast."

So he went down a narrow hallway and right up to the double doors that always indicated the office of the Big Cheese and he kept right on going, right on through the doors. What he saw then startled him.

Michael Dailey stood in the middle of his office with Jane Dunphy in his arms.

"Jesus!" Dailey snapped.

But Tobin could say nothing. Only stare. Jane broke from Dailey's embrace. Tobin had never seen her look lovelier or more alien. He could not imagine her kissing somebody like Dailey. Could not fucking fathom it.

"Just what the hell are you doing?" Dailey said. He

106

wore a gray pinstripe suit so smartly tailored it resembled a dinner outfit.

"I need to talk to you." But he couldn't keep his eyes from Jane's face. He felt so confused and angry and despairing.

"Then make an appointment."

"I don't have time for an appointment."

Finally, finally she spoke. Her soft voice both soothed and chilled Tobin. It was over between them and he had acknowledged that months ago, but—Michael Dailey? "I really should be going anyway."

"I'm sorry this happened," Dailey said.

"It's all right." She glanced at him and wrinkled her mouth in a little smile and then she glanced at Tobin and he thought for a moment he saw something like shame move across her face, but then she put on a smile identical to the one she'd just given Dailey and started out of the office. Today she wore a blue jumper with a white blouse and her hair was pinned up with a sweet little pink barrette. She belonged in the suburbs, for Christ's sake, not here in the clutches of a leading theatrical vampire. What was going on?

"I'll call you," Dailey said and he made it sound proprietary, husband-to-wife.

"All right," she said, and was gone.

In the ensuing silence—Dailey obviously taking pleasure in Tobin's shock—Tobin looked dully around the office. A window half as wide as the wall showed the windows of nearby office buildings. From the street below came the distant sounds of Christmas music.

Dailey went around behind his desk, neat and tidy as *Forbes* would recommend, and said, "I'm giving you exactly two minutes."

"I have a list."

"Good for you. So do I. It's Christmas time. A lot of

people have lists at Christmas time."

"I have a list of people who might be considered serious suspects in Richard's death."

"Perhaps you haven't heard, Tobin. The police consider you suspect number one."

"That's strange, Michael. Suspect number one on my list is you."

"Me?"

"You were cheating him."

Dailey surprised him by laughing. While he unconsciously played with his solid-gold cuff links (which were big enough to clog up drains), he also put on his best Cesar Romero smile and said, "You've been talking to Starrett."

"He says he has proof."

"He doesn't have a damn thing except a bad case of envy. He wanted to be Richard's exclusive representative for the screenplay. He's just angry that Richard let me handle all the details."

"Why didn't I hear about this screenplay until yesterday?"

"Gosh, Tobin, I wasn't aware that either Richard or I had to keep you informed of our activities."

"Richard and I used to be good friends. The best friends."

"Until you started mooching a free ride."

"Bullshit. We each brought things to the show."

"Richard sold a novel. You didn't. Richard, thanks in part to my own talents as a publicist, had very high visibility—you didn't. Now there's a screenplay. Some very big names on the Coast are interested in starring in it." He smirked. "How's your career been going lately?"

Tobin couldn't stop himself. "Are you sure Richard wrote that screenplay?"

For the first time that morning, Dailey seemed uncertain of himself. "What's that supposed to mean?"

"Just what I said."

"Of course he wrote it."

"Do you know anything about a man named Ebsen?"

This time Dailey tried to laugh but couldn't quite manage to make the sound. "That creep."

"So you know him?"

"Richard told me about him. He was a student of Richard's."

"He seems to be hinting that he had something to do with writing the screenplay."

"He's a liar."

Tobin smiled. "I'd like to see you call him that to his face, Michael. You'd keep that plastic surgeon you represent busy for several weeks in the operating room."

"Richard wrote the screenplay."

"Ebsen says he's going to the press unless he's paid a certain sum of money."

"I know. He's been pestering Jane."

Again Tobin couldn't help himself. "You don't have any right to be with her. The man is only one day dead."

"Her being married didn't seem to bother you any when you were having your affair."

Tobin knew he was blushing.

"For shit's sake, Tobin, do you think it was a secret? Richard knew all along. He thought it would be good for Jane. She hadn't taken his fame very well—felt very much left behind. Especially when she began to sense that Richard was seeing a lot of other women, which happened to be the case. Did her good to have somebody pay special attention to her. Even if it had to be you."

There was nothing to say, of course. He felt embarrassed and hollowed out and betrayed by everybody involved, including Jane herself, who now had some indeterminate relationship with Dailey here.

Tobin went back to the reason he'd come here. "Starrett will demand an audit of the books."

"He can demand anything he wants. It doesn't mean he'll get it."

A buzz on the intercom. Discreet as the earth tones. "Mr. Dailey, it's the Coast."

"The Coast. Good." Dailey nodded to the phone. "That concludes the interview part of our show," he said to Tobin. "Don't think it hasn't been fun."

"Let me give you a word of advice. If you're playing games with Harold Ebsen, you'd better be careful. He's a very dangerous guy."

Dailey smiled. "Thanks so much, Tobin. You know how much I value advice coming from you."

Tobin left.

18 1:04 P.M.

Jeff Bridges said, "It isn't my fault I'm cross-eyed." Then he crossed his eyes and made Helen Slater, who had previously been mad at him, laugh. It was good teaming, Bridges and Slater (God, but she had a good clean beautiful uncomplicated face), and for a time Tobin sat in the darkness of the screening room dreaming teenage dreams again (all about meeting Helen Slater and being puppy-love happy walking down the golden winter streets with her). And then it was all over, the credits rolling while the rock tie-in song played, and he knew it had been a good movie (a murder mystery set in an advertising agency) because he didn't want it to end.

In the lobby afterward, Chamales came up and offered himself yet again as Tobin's TV partner. Tobin said, "We'll have to look into that, won't we?" Then a critic named Swenson who did pieces on action stars for magazines that featured the trade secrets of gore movies' special effects appeared. As always, he was dressed in a bush jacket and wore mirror sunglasses. He was a half inch shorter than Tobin. A bloody goddamn midget.

"Piece of shit," he said.

"I'm giving it four stars," Tobin said.

"I'm going to give it five," Chamales said, patting his girth, which was today swaddled in a red turtleneck sweater that gave him the appearance of a globe on legs.

"Pretentious," Swenson said. "Too much talk."

"Believe it or not, Swenson, more people talk than get into car chases or get chased by monsters," Tobin said.

"At least they could have had more cleavage," Swenson said.

All Tobin could do was shake his head. In a column once (true story) Swenson had attacked Fellini's *Amarcord* as a perfect example of why the United States shouldn't import movies but should only "show things produced right here in the good ole U.S.A." He had gone on to say that *Amarcord* could have used a little "Roger Corman magic." Tobin assumed that some night he and Swenson would get drunk together and then Tobin would beat his fucking face in.

111

"So how do you think you're going to like your new boss?"

Tobin said, "What new boss?"

"Pennco. You mean you haven't heard? Emory's selling the company to them," Swenson said. Pennco was the second-largest television syndicator in the world.

He hadn't heard about the movie script. He hadn't heard about Michael Dailey and Jane Dunphy being lovers. And now he hadn't heard about Frank Emory, whom he considered not only a boss but a friend, selling the company.

"You sure?"

"Hell, yes. It's all over the bars." Swenson smiled. "Pennco is wall-to-wall assholes."

"So I've heard."

"Maybe I can get you some gigs on the magazines I work for. In case things don't work out for you, I mean."

Tobin saw that, even though they didn't get along, Swenson was seriously trying to help him. Then of course Tobin felt like shit for thinking all those rotten things about Swenson who, despite his execrable taste in films, had turned out to be a rare type of person—a charitable man.

"Maybe I'll take you up on that," Tobin said. But he was strictly on autopilot. His mind was imploding. Jane having an affair with Dailey. Frank Emory selling the company.

"Well, I'm kind of late for an appointment," Tobin muttered. "I'll see you later."

"Have a good holiday," Chamales said.

Tobin clapped them both on the shoulders—as if they were the best friends he had in the world (as they damn well might be, considering everything that was going on)—then found the elevators and went downstairs.

"I take it you know who this is?" Neely said.

"Sure he does," Huggins said.

Neely said, "I've been calling all over fuck for you, Tobin. Huggins here has been trying to locate you."

This was a wonderful place for a conversation. Right outside the Brill Building. Freezing your ass off. People walking by and staring. And a Santa Claus with hostile eyes thinking hostile thoughts about everybody who passed by him. Ho-fucking-ho.

"I've got some bad news for you, Tobin," Huggins said. He still looked like Frog Face McGraw, though you wouldn't have thought Frog Face was the kind of kid who would grow up to wear blue cashmere topcoats and spend the cost of a good dinner at the Four Seasons on a haircut.

"Gee, that's what I'd like. Some more bad news."

"He thinks he's broken your alibi," Neely said. "That's why I wanted to be here."

"Shut up," Huggins said to Neely. "I'm doing the talking."

Neely gave Huggins his best kicked-dog expression and then over his shoulder flashed a little yellow thing he had in his hand and sort of waved it at Tobin. Great, Tobin thought. I'm standing here getting busted by a cop and my frigging lawyer is toking on a joint.

Neely took some marijuana in deep and then expelled it with great luxury. He smiled a 1968 smile at Tobin.

Huggins faced Tobin, so he saw none of this. "After talking with the stagehand and with Jane Dunphy," he said, "I realized there was a fairly long period there when you were alone. The first time I interviewed the stagehand, he tried to make it sound like you were alone just a minute or two."

"So?"

113

"So you could easily have gone down the hall to your dressing room and stabbed him."

"And just why would I do this?"

Huggins shook his sleek head. "Are you shitting me, Tobin? You really wonder if we got you on motive?" He counted the motives off on his calfskin-gloved fingers. "One, he wouldn't sign his contract—and that would put you out on the street. Two, you were having an affair with his wife. Three, you'd gotten into an argument with him that was so bad you punched it out while the tape rolled."

All Neely did was take another toke and sort of shrug at Tobin as if to say, He made some good points, you gotta give him that, some good points.

"So you're arresting me?"

"Not yet."

"Why not?"

"Because Frank Emory's father is important and Frank talked his father into calling a friend at the Mayor's office." He smiled. "But you've seen a lot of cop movies, Tobin. So you know better than to leave town, right?"

Tobin sighed. "Right."

Huggins merged with Frog Face again. "I'm going to nail you, Tobin. Nail you real good."

With that, he turned, glared at both of them, and stalked dramatically back to his unmarked Pontiac sitting at the curb.

"What a dumb fuck," Neely said. "He didn't even know I had a joint."

"You were a big help. Thanks a lot."

"Hey, I told you I was a shitty lawyer," Neely said earnestly.

Tobin shook his head. "I guess I should have believed you, shouldn't I?"

19

Tobin had always envied Richard Dunphy his house (not to mention, for a time, his wife). The three-story white clapboard sat on a dead-end street that wound up through fir trees and pines. You had the sense of isolation, but your nearest neighbor was no farther away than an eighth of a mile.

Now, as the cab pulled up the curving driveway, Tobin saw a snowman, arms wide in greeting, carrot nose and coal-piece smile, a red stocking cap on its head, standing in front of the house. For the first time since Richard's death, he thought not of himself and his own problems with the police and with his future career, but of the children involved. He was their godfather and he hadn't given them a thought.

Walking up to the long, screened-in porch, redolent always for Tobin of the late fifties when you sat through summer afternoons of Ray Bradbury and Isaac Asimov paperbacks and drank lemonade or a bottle of Pepsi that still only cost ten cents. But now there was snow and frost on the porch and it was a long way from the relative innocence of the fifties.

When she opened the door for him he could see that she hadn't gotten much sleep and he could smell that she'd had more than a little to drink. She wore one of Dunphy's blue cardigans (he'd worn blue cardigans

115

since their college days) and a white blouse and loose jeans and she still managed, in her suburban way, to look very pretty. "Hello, Tobin." She didn't open the door.

"I'd like to come in."

"I'm not sure that's a good idea."

"I really need to talk."

"There was a report on the news—a very broad hint—that you might be implicated in Richard's death. The kids saw it." She winced. "I'm not sure now would be a good time for them to see you."

"Please. I need to ask you a few questions."

She smiled. "Playing detective?"

"I don't have much choice, do I? The police aren't even seriously considering any other suspects."

She assessed him, then said, "Do you think I might have done it?"

He looked at the floor and then he looked back up. "I don't know."

"You *do* think I'm a suspect."

"At this point, everybody's a suspect."

"Thank you very much."

"You're not at the top or anything, though."

"The top?"

He patted his pocket. "The top of my list. I'm making a list of all the potential suspects. You're near the bottom."

Without humor, she joked, "That's a relief."

He couldn't stop what he said next. "I can't believe you're involved with Michael Dailey."

For the first time, she averted her blue eyes. When she looked back up at him, she sighed. Then she opened the door and held it back so he could walk in.

There was a Christmas tree wide enough to fill an entire corner of the large living room, with spangly tin-

sel and flashing red and blue and green lights and beatific white angels and a long line of reindeer. Spread
around the bottom of the tree were piles of presents,
some wrapped with great solemn formality (Bloom-
ingdale's, Neiman Marcus, Carson Pirie Scott), others
obviously done with the haste and inexeperience of a
child's hand. But he did not need to ask what present
the two kids would want most for this Christmas—their
father.

She saw him looking around and said, "They're up
in the hills with their sleds."

"Oh."

"It's none of your business, Tobin."

"Michael?"

"Right. Michael."

"So you won't talk about it?"

This time she only shrugged. "You want some Irish
coffee? That's what I'm having."

"No. I need to be very sober."

"Sure?"

"Sure."

"I didn't kill him," she said.

"I don't really think you did."

"Then why are you here?"

"For one thing, I'd like to see a copy of that script, if
you've got it."

"Oh, yes, the script."

"You sound bitter about it."

"It's not the script that makes me bitter. It's all the
grief the script caused."

"What grief?"

"For one thing, a man named Ebsen."

"I met him this morning. Nice guy."

"He's a sick man." As he watched her, he saw an
edge he'd never known her to have before—a certain

hardness. Then he recognized it for what it really was. She was uncomfortable around him. They'd slept together a hundred times, he'd held her head while she vomited, she'd eased his grief the night he burned his screenplay and swore off writing anything but criticism (a bad and dangerous night, that). And now she was uncomfortable around him.

"I got that impression," Tobin said.

"He claims that Richard took the draft of a script he wrote and changed it a little, then sold it himself."

"Do you think that's possible?"

She stared at him directly. "As you suggested a few minutes ago, Tobin—anything's possible."

"He wants money."

"I know. He's called here three times today already."

"He says he'll go to the press with the story if he doesn't get his money by six."

"Do you know how much he wants?"

"No."

"A hundred thousand dollars." She smiled and in that moment she was the woman he'd loved for so many years. It was her absurd smile, the one that said the world was just too unbelievable to cope with. "He seems to think I keep that much cash in my cookie jar."

He laughed. "You mean you don't?"

It was the right thing to say, and the right way to say it, because she came into his arms almost before he was through speaking. "Oh, God, Tobin, it's so fucked up."

He let her cry.

"It's all right," he said at one point, stroking the back of her head. They used to be good at that with each other—comfort and succor, he the Daddy one night, she the Mommy the next.

When she stopped crying, she pulled back and

looked him in the face and said, "Is my nose running?"

"No. But it's very red."

She laughed. "Red I can live with." She sort of snuffled and then angled her head and looked out through the big window on the side at the firs that sloped all the way up to the horizon line in the bright sunlight outdoors. "You want me to tell you about Michael?"

"You don't have to."

"But you want me to."

"I guess I'm curious, if that's what you mean."

"He's actually got a nice side."

He sighed. "I just realized something."

"What?"

"You really do care about him, don't you?"

She nodded.

"Boy, maybe this won't be so much fun to hear."

She touched his cheek. Gently. "Then let's talk about something else."

But of course he had a lover's terrible fascination for the worst news of all. "How did it happen?"

"It started at a party."

"Why Michael?"

"Because you and I were long past any kind of relationship and because Richard had stopped coming home completely, thanks to Sarah Nichols, and because I saw Michael hurt very deeply one night. At the party, I mean."

"What happened?"

"He found his wife Joan in the back seat of the car with Peter Larson. Making love. It was like high school. And Michael—just sort of came apart."

"Michael?"

"Yes. I know the veneer he's cultivated—very slick and indifferent. But actually he's not that way at all."

"So you played Mommy."

"You're being sarcastic."

"I'm jealous."

She touched his cheek again. "You're not jealous. You're just confused. We used each other as kind of a buffer against the world—you kept me from facing just how bad my marriage was, I kept you from realizing how lonely you are, Tobin. You're a very lonely and angry man and the problem is, I don't think there's anything anybody can do for you about that. Anybody. Even yourself, Tobin, and that's the saddest part of all."

He looked around at the Christmas tree and the comfortable living room and realized she was right. "Goddamn, but I loved you when we were rolling there."

"And I really loved you, too."

"But now you love Michael?"

"I'm not sure what I feel—yet."

"What's he going to do about Joan?"

"Oh, she's safely in the arms of Peter Larson." She laughed. "The funny thing is, I think both of us got together partially out of spite."

"What do you mean?"

"We both thought Joan and Richard were having an affair. There was a period of a month or so when they were inseparable."

He thought back and then he remembered that, yes, there had been a time six or seven months ago when Joan was around the studios a great deal.

"One night after you'd taped a show where Richard was particularly laudatory about one of Peter Larson's films, she even called here to thank him. I thought she had a lot of guts."

"I think the word you want is balls."

"Yeah," she laughed, "that is a better word. Balls." She shrugged. "But as it turned out, anyway, the person she was having an affair with was Peter Larson, her boss."

"She works for Larson now?"

"Yes. You didn't know that?"

"No."

He patted his pocket and took out the wrinkled piece of paper that had become so important to him. In addition to names, he had also started writing down one-word memory-joggers.

"That's your list?"

"Right."

"It's not very impressive. Don't policemen carry reporter's notebooks and flip the covers back when they start an interview?"

"I'm not really a cop. Just a junior G-man."

"That explains a lot."

He smiled and looked at his list. "Did Ebsen ever mention anything to you about reviews?"

"What reviews?"

"I'm not sure. When I was at his place today he said something to the effect that I didn't know what was going on with the reviews. I don't know what that means."

"Neither do I."

"You think I could take a copy of the script?"

"Sure. If you like. There's one in the den."

While she went to get it, he walked over to the Christmas tree. He thought of his mother and father and then of his own children. It was one of those moments when a man tries to make sense of his life and how badly he's lived it; it was one of those moments when his existence made no sense whatsoever.

"Here."

The script was in a nice black leather cover. He hefted it, then leafed through it. "Thanks. Oh. One more question."

"What?"

"Starrett says Michael was embezzling from Richard. Did you hear anything about that?"

"Richard found a note that Michael wrote me. Right after that, all this talk of embezzlement came up. Michael and Richard were going to formally end their relationship next month, when Richard tried to get a new show for himself."

"That isn't how Michael acted the night Richard was killed. He didn't give any hint they weren't getting along."

"He didn't have much choice. You don't exactly walk around broadcasting that your biggest client has left you." Then she paused and said, "I see where this is leading."

"I have to put Michael on my list."

"He didn't kill him."

He sighed, looking at her in a kind of disbelief. He recognized her expression, had seen it many times. Love. Her very own kind of protective love. Only now it was not for him or for Richard but for that most unlikely and undeserving man, Michael. Tobin stood in her living room and felt invisible worlds crashing in on him. No one is more of a stranger than someone who loved you once but loves you no longer. A burdensome sadness came over him—for both of them—and he said quietly, "He still needs to go on the list, Jane. At least for now."

"I don't think I want you here anymore."

"I know."

"Are we even friends now?"

"I'm not sure."

"Do I need to see you to the door?"

"No," he said. "No, you don't."

Then he was gone.

20   5:17 P.M.

There was champagne. Real champagne. There were party hats. There were pink and yellow and blue streamers and confetti of a thousand colors. And there were women—bloody Christ, but were there women. Some with fetching faces. Some with beguiling breasts. Some with asses that winked and some with asses that frowned. There was enough laughter to fill an NFL locker room after a winning Superbowl and enough bullshit patter to keep Vegas (Hiya/Loveya/ Kissya) in business for a year. There was a party going on at Emory Communications and Tobin did not need to ask why. Frank Emory had sold his way out of failure.

"Tobin. Goddamn—Tobin!"

Frank was drunk and kind of squatting down and holding his arms wide as if Tobin were going to come running into them. Despite the dignity his height and gray hair and preppy manner should have given him, he was anything but dignified now. This was Frank at his worst. Trying to be one of the boys. He was as bad at it as Tobin.

"Hi, Frank."

"'Hi, Frank.' That's all I get on the biggest day of my life?"

"Congratulations."

"At the least, buddy-boy. At the frigging least."

"Don't call me buddy-boy, all right?"

"Jesus, did you come up here to queer my party?"

"Actually, I came up to ask you a few questions. I didn't know you were having a party."

Frank sloshed champagne. "That's all I'm going to do for the next six months. Party. Party my ass off."

His wife, who had been kissing cheeks, turned to Tobin and said, "Make that plural. Party our asses off." She beamed. "Aren't you proud of him?"

"For selling out?"

"For selling out for a profit, Tobin. For a profit. That's what's important," she said.

"A big profit, Tobin," Frank said. "A goddamn big profit."

So there was no talking to him, not now anyway, so Tobin circulated, hearing tales of adultery and business betrayals and careering and the latest suspected AIDS victim and watching old men try to steal quick feels from young women, and watching young women try to cajole better jobs from old men. He stood by the Christmas tree and looked out over Manhattan, the night a crypt, his lungs raw from cigarette smoke, his mind fixed on misery, Jane's look there at the last, Huggins's trying to prove him a killer, Neely never growing up.

"I'm sorry I was so rude."

Sarah Nichols, looking more the Irish beauty than ever, touched his arm. There was no doubting what Richard had seen in her. Why he'd spent more and more time with her. Her eyes, her hazel eyes, cast you in their grace and you never wanted to leave. "Out at the college, I mean."

"It's all right."

"No, it isn't. I was just upset. I don't really think you killed him."

"Then you seem to be in the minority."

"The police still suspect you?"

"I'm afraid they do."

"Well, anyway, I just wanted to come over and say I was sorry."

"I accept."

"Thank you."

She turned to leave.

He said, on a whim really, half serious about his question but at least half motivated by the tidal power of those hazel eyes, "Do you know a man named Ebsen at the college?"

"Harold Ebsen. Sure. Everybody does."

"Then you probably know what he says about Richard?"

"That Richard stole his screenplay?"

"Yes."

"He's been saying that for months."

"Is it true?"

She surprised him. "I don't know."

"You mean you think there's a chance Richard actually cribbed his screenplay?"

"Oh, not cribbed it exactly. Took something that was very primitive, perhaps, and improved it. Improved it a great deal."

"Do you think Ebsen would have killed him over it?"

"I have absolutely no doubt Ebsen would have killed him over it. After he followed us around with that shotgun microphone, I wouldn't put anything past him."

"Shotgun microphone?"

"A few months ago, when he really began pestering Richard and me, he started following us everywhere with a shotgun microphone he stole from the school's production department. Then the next day he'd drop off the tape in Richard's office. Obviously it gave him a great sense of power."

"But you never heard him actually threaten Richard?"

"Threaten him physically, you mean?"

"Right."

"Not actually, no. But with somebody like him, that's always there implicitly." She nodded with her lovely head. "Here's your friend." She looked matronly suddenly—sixty-year-old disapproval on the face of a young woman. Something was going on behind him that displeased her.

He turned to see Frank Emory doing a kind of dirty boogie, legs flailing, to a disco song that was blasting out of wall speakers.

"Richard always said he was a silly ass. He wasn't wrong."

Then Frank was with them and throwing his arm around Tobin and kind of pressing his head against Tobin's head and spilling champagne everywhere. "Am I drunk, or what?"

"You're very drunk," Sarah Nichols said. "Inexcusably drunk, as a matter of fact."

She went away.

"She never liked me."

"Right now you're sort of hard to like."

"You don't like me? My old friend Tobin doesn't like me on the happiest night of my life?"

"The night you got married—the nights your kids were born—one of those should have been the happiest night of your life. Not this, Frank. This just means you couldn't take the heat anymore and you gave up."

Tobin saw how badly he'd hurt him and for just a

moment he took at least some small pleasure from the pain he'd inflicted, but then he saw Frank's face—the jaw coming open, the drunken blue eyes go dead—and then he knew he'd had no right to say that, no matter how true it might be.

"Jesus, Frank, I'm going to go."

Frank's tears were obvious. "I thought we were friends."

"We are." And this time it was Tobin who threw his arm around Frank. (Not easy, given Tobin's height.) "We're goddamn good friends, and I had no right to say it. I don't blame you a damn bit. I would have done the same thing myself as soon as Richard was killed. I have to put my ego aside and just look at the facts. Without the team, there was no show."

Frank managed to recapture at least some of his previous luster. He slurred his words but he seemed to be having a good time slurring his words. "Actually, my friend, I started negotiating for the sale several months ago."

"Really?"

Frank pawed the front of his blue blazer. "Right. This whole process has taken months." He said "processessh" and "shtaken."

"And you didn't tell anybody?"

"Just my wife."

"So they wanted our show then?'

"They wanted your show very much. The papers were signed two days ago—before Richard was killed." He shook his head. Lowered his voice. Leaned in. "Goddamn, Tobin, I'll be honest with you. I just lucked out is all. If Richard had been murdered before those papers were signed—" His eyes grew miserable again. "There wouldn't have been any sale, buddy-boy, no sale at all."

"I'm glad it worked out for you, Frank. I really am."

He was overdoing it, overcompensating really, for being such a jerk. Then he said, "I wanted to ask you about a man named Ebsen."

Frank grinned, leaned in again. "Don't ask me about men, ask me about women." He whispered. "Did you see that secretary from the second floor?" He said, ". . . she that shecretary from the shecond floor."

"Yeah."

"With the boobs?"

"Yeah."

"Out to here?"

"Right."

"Out to fucking *here*?"

There was no point talking to Frank. Not tonight.

"Well," Tobin said.

"You sound like you're leaving."

Tobin feigned a yawn. "I'm tired. Been a very hard twenty-four hours, Frank."

"Christ, don't leave."

"I'd really better."

He threw his arms wide again. "We're having a party. A fucking party." Then he shrugged. "I mean, I know it's pretty soon after Richard's death."

"Almost forty-eight hours."

"Don't get sarcastic again."

Tobin sighed. "There's no reason not to have a party, Frank. It's a big night for you, as you say. Life goes on."

"Life goes fucking on. Right on," Frank said.

"Well," Tobin said again in that preparatory tone. Three minutes and twenty-two seconds later he was in the elevator.

21
She moved out of the shadows of his apartment house doorway.

"Hi."

"God, how long you been standing here?"

"Not long."

"How long is not long?"

"Half an hour."

"Half an hour? Christ."

"Some men would take that as flattery. You seem angry about it."

He realized she was right. He was still back there at the Emory party. All the people. All the bullshit.

"Maybe we should start again," Tobin said.

"Huh?"

'You say 'hi' again and this time I'll try not to be such a big prick."

"That sounds like fun. 'Hi.'"

It was exactly the kind of lovemaking Tobin needed. Passionate at first to work off some energy and rid himself of his anger, then slower and more gentle with those half-words that are more tones than meanings, soothing tones as he worshiped in her grotto once again, and then she took him inside and cradled him when he was finished, stroking him, whispering more

129

half-words, then saying, "There isn't anything more beautiful, is there?"

"What?"

"A Christmas tree in the darkness."

"I wish it were a bigger tree. For your sake, I mean."

"It's a fine tree, Tobin."

He was coming out of her anyway (the Little Sizzler had sizzled its last for a time) and then he lay beside her and watched the shadows cast in the bedroom by the tree lights.

"Did you ever want a present and not get it?" Marcie asked.

"Sure."

"What was it?"

"Cowboy boots. I was a real Roy Rogers fan when I was six. So I wrote Santa Claus a letter and said, 'Look you son of a bitch, I really mean business about this, I want 'em or you're dead meat.' And so, naturally, in that playful way of his, he told me to get stuffed. He brought me a truck, a homely little red truck, and I'd hardly gotten it unwrapped when my baby brother came along and sat on it and broke the hell out of it."

Her laughter was wonderful there in the bedroom.

"How about you?" he said. "What did you want especially that you never got?"

"A bra. When I was thirteen. Except I got it."

"And you were still unhappy?"

"Yeah, because as soon as I got it I put it on but it wouldn't stay up. I didn't have any breasts."

"You've got nice ones now."

"Not big ones, though."

"Nice ones. Beautiful ones."

"Gee, I wish I could stay longer and listen to all this praise."

"You serious? You have to go?"

"I wish I could stay longer." She sighed. "I have to.

130

Tomorrow's Christmas Eve, and my mother always gets pretty bad—her melancholy over my father, I mean."

He knew, given those circumstances, there was nothing he could say that wouldn't just be selfish. He said, "Maybe you could stay just an other hour or so."

"I wish I could."

"I have no pride. I'll get down and beg."

She laughed again and again it was wonderful. "You're a strange guy, Tobin, you really are. Half of you is so nice."

"And the other half?"

She kissed him on the nose. "Well, not as nice as the other half."

The phone rang and he looked at it first as an interruption, then decided he'd better answer it. He reached across her for the receiver, kissing her on the way.

"Tobin?"

"Yes."

Pause. "This is Harold Ebsen."

Tobin frowned. "I talked to Jane Dunphy. I don't think you're going to get your money." He paused. Ebsen was a sleazy bastard, no doubt about that, but given Sarah Nichols's comments earlier, maybe Dunphy really had lifted a part of Ebsen's screenplay. So he decided to give Ebsen a Christmas gift of some good advice. "Quit threatening people. Contact a lawyer, a good one, and institute a lawsuit. If you've got any kind of proof at all, Dunphy's estate will probably make an out-of-court settlement. Happens all the time."

There was traffic noise in the background. Horns especially. Ebsen said something but obviously he was calling from a phone booth outdoors. Tobin couldn't hear him.

"Can you speak up?"

"I said I've got something for you."

"What?"

"Some interesting information."

"Like what?"

"Like maybe I know who really killed Dunphy."

"Who would that be?"

"Well, he had a wife, a mistress, and an agent who was screwing him. For just three people."

Tobin thought of being followed around by a creep with a shotgun microphone. A creep gathering data on your life. By now Ebsen probably knew as much about Dunphy as anybody did.

"So how do I get this information?"

"I'll bring it to you around ten o'clock tonight. For three thousand dollars."

"That's a long way from what you were asking before."

"Maybe I'd better split town. I need cash."

"I can't get three thousand dollars cash tonight."

"I can get your check cashed."

Tobin sighed. "If you know something, you should go to the police. Ask for a Detective Huggins."

Ebsen said, "You think he'd give me three grand?"

"Ebsen, look, I—"

"See you tonight."

He hung up.

"That was Harold Ebsen?" she said. She was over by the chair where she'd laid her jeans and sweater, getting dressed. In the Christmas-tree lights, her young body was more lovely than ever. "The creep?"

"He sure seems to have a lot of fans."

"He doesn't deserve any fans. Not after what he did to Dunphy."

"I heard. About the shotgun microphone?"

"Oh, not just that, Tobin. Not just that. He even started following Dunphy's friends around. He sent several of them cassette tapes that read 'With compliments of Richard Dunphy.'"

"Why would he start taping people?"

"Power."

"Power?"

"When you start following people around—and he followed a lot of people and audio-taped them—then you have power. Or you think you do. Sometimes he'd just tape people indiscriminately."

Tobin sat up in bed. "How do you know all this stuff?"

"I heard Dunphy and him arguing in Dunphy's office one night. Dunphy sounded ready to punch him out."

"Why didn't Dunphy go to the police?"

She shrugged. "I guess I couldn't help you there."

"I guess I'll find out tonight."

"He wants money from you, doesn't he?"

"Three thousand dollars."

"That creep. He really is." She glanced at her watch. "Well, I'd really better be going. Mom's baking cookies tonight. She likes having me sit in the kitchen with her and smell them bake. She says it reminds her of when I was a little girl." She smiled. "Sometimes it makes me smile."

"Your red mittens make me smile," Tobin said, going over in his underwear and kissing her tenderly.

"My red mittens?"

"Red knit mittens. Little-girl red knit mittens. They're sweet."

She held them up for his inspection. "This is what my mom does when she's not baking cookies."

Then she returned his kiss. "I'll call you tomorrow, Tobin. Just be careful with Ebsen. I wouldn't trust him at all."

"Funny," Tobin said, "I got the same impression for some reason."

22

11:26 P.M.

After Marcie Pierce had left, Tobin worked out on his rowing machine, took a shower, and then put *The Lady in Red* on the VCR. He was writing a piece on John Sayles for *American Film* and he considered the Sayles script for *Lady* his absolute best.

Then it was time for Harold Ebsen to show up.

Tobin paced around the large, drafty apartment. Several times tonight he had considered calling Detective Huggins and telling him all the things he'd learned in the past twenty-four hours—but he knew that Huggins would offer no help in following up leads. He already had his killer—Tobin.

Around eleven-thirty Tobin, curious and tense now from the waiting, decided to go downstairs to the vestibule to see if the bell was out of order or something.

When he reached the vestibule, the door was flung back and the young married couple from across the hall came tripping in under the burden of their Christmas packages. Tobin stuck his head out the door—looked left and right, seeing nothing—then helped the couple carry some of their load upstairs.

Back in his apartment, he looked up Harold Ebsen's phone number in the book and dialed it. Busy. He went in the john and whizzed and came back and tried again. Still busy. For some reason Harold Ebsen had decided not to keep his appointment.

Tobin needed to know why.

134

23 Friday 12:23 A.M.

"I'll be right back," Tobin told the cabdriver.

Even the Christmas decorations on Ebsen's street were dark this time of night. Tobin got out of the cab, drawing his topcoat collar up around him. It was three degrees above zero.

There had been a snowfall earlier tonight, so Ebsen's unshoveled walk was slicker than it had been the past morning. He inched along, staring ahead at the small house. It was as black as the rest of the street. If Ebsen was on the phone, why were there no lights?

Tobin went up and tried to peer through the painted-over windows, but that was useless. Then he stood on tiptoe and tried to look in through the front door. That proved hopeless too.

He decided to do the unlikely thing, knock.

He raised his hand and brought it down in a sharp knock.

He was surprised by the sound of something being scraped across the bare wood floor inside.

His knock had apparently startled somebody who had inadvertently made a noise.

He stood there, his nostrils getting frosty, shrinking inside his topcoat from the cold. He listened very carefully for any other evidence of somebody inside, but there was nothing. Then he got an idea and carefully made his way off the porch and down the walk and back into the cab.

"Back home?" the cabbie asked.

"No. Around the block. Then go in the alley."

He watched the cabbie's eyes fill the rearview mirror. "You sure?"

"I'm sure."

"I don't want no trouble."

"There won't be any." Tobin smiled. "It's my wife. I think she's got a boyfriend."

"Long as the boyfriend doesn't have a gun."

"He's her hairdresser."

"Oh, hell, then. No sweat." Here was a guy who obviously believed everything he read in the *Post*.

All the way around the block Tobin wished he could just stay in the back seat of the cab. It felt safe and warm in here. The glow of the dashboard lights. The radio low with Nat "King" Cole's beautiful "Christmas Song." The houses that were so shabby during the day were now almost beautiful, tucked in against a backdrop of snow. If he never had to leave the cab, he could spend the rest of his life happily just riding around, maybe coast to coast, or maybe somebody would build a highway across the ocean and he could visit London and Paris, just sitting in the back of the cab, safe from Detective Huggins and safe from his past.

"Here we are," the cabbie said.

The alley was a tunnel formed by long flanks of tiny one-stall garages, many of which leaned dramatically left or right in various stages of collapse. The moonlight here seemed bright.

"Now we wait."

"You think she's gonna come out the back?"

"She'll have to."

"Why?"

"There's her car."

And so there was. A car. A new gray Mercedes se-
dan. Parked at an angle in front of Ebsen's closed one-
stall garage. He knew, of course, who owned the car.

"Think I'll have some coffee. If I had an empty cup,
I'd offer you one," the cabbie said.

"That's fine. I'm going in."

"You going to walk in on them?"

"Isn't that the best way?"

"Man, I don't know. Seeing your old lady all tangled
up in somebody else's bed. Man, I don't know if you
could ever get that sight out of your mind."

"It's the only way," Tobin said solemnly.

"Well, good luck."

"Thanks."

So Tobin got out and started up to the house. The
moonlight cast long shadows from a naked elm. Wind
whipped up a fine silty snow that was not unlike frozen
cocaine. He was cold within a minute of leaving the cab.

On his way he saw a fenced-in area of chicken wire
with what appeared to be an oversized doghouse ap-
pended to the garage. This was where Ebsen kept his
chickens. They were down for the night. Abreast of
their house he smelled chicken droppings on the stark
night air.

The back porch looked as if it had been stuck on as
an afterthought. He tried the screen door and found it
open and so then, carefully, carefully, he eased his way
up the steps and onto the porch. There were enough
beer cases stacked up to start your own Budweiser
warehouse.

Then he tripped over a garden rake that had apparently fallen down earlier. He crashed against the beer
cases. Glass bottles rattled. As in sympathy, something
inside the house fell, too.

Tobin stood in the ensuing silence, his heart a wild

animal in his chest, no longer cold but sweating. Waiting.

He was still waiting when the inside back door opened and a tall man in a continental-cut coat stood there dramatically with a pistol in his hand.

"Jesus," Tobin said. "Are you crazy?"

"I don't want any of your bullshit, Tobin. Something terrible has happened here."

"What?"

Michael Dailey gulped, his handsome, actorish face almost statue-like now that it was not animated either by superiority or malice. He sounded distant, a bit in shock. "Somebody killed Ebsen."

"That wouldn't have been you, Michael, would it?"

"I didn't kill him, Tobin. I promise."

"Where is he?"

Dailey turned. Tobin followed. One step across the threshold the smells of the slaughterhouse were back. In the thin moonlight through the frosty window and falling across the floor he saw feathers and splotches of blood. Somehow he didn't think he'd ever feel at home here.

Ebsen was sprawled across the living-room floor. He'd exchanged his T-shirt for a white shirt that looked as though he'd laid it under a freshly killed chicken. The way he was twisted, he might have been a tot fallen asleep watching TV.

"Shot," Michael Dailey said, as if he needed to explain the situation to Tobin.

"I sort of guessed that."

"Did you kill him, Tobin?"

"Don't try it, Michael."

"What?"

"Trying to convince me that you can implicate me. I'm going over there to the phone and calling the po-

138

lice, Detective Huggins, to be exact, and I'm going to tell them exactly what I found here."

"God, Tobin, listen, I really didn't do it. Please. Here, look, I'll even give you the gun." When he leaned forward, his white silk scarf fell loose. His Valentino-slick hair glistened.

"No, thanks, Michael. I'd just as soon not have my fingerprints on it."

He'd never seen Michael lose his composure before. He sort of enjoyed it.

"Then what were you doing here?"

"I—" Now he was the old Michael again. His eyes became hooded and inscrutable. "I just needed to do something. But I didn't kill him."

"Not good enough. Either you tell me what you were doing here or I call Huggins."

"You'll just use it to destroy him. You'll just use it to build yourself up."

"I don't know what you're talking about."

"Dammit, Tobin, don't make me tell you. Please. It won't do anybody any good."

"Does it have to do with the script Richard sold?"

"No."

This surprised Tobin. "Then why else would you be here?"

"Because there's a—book deal pending. I'd been planning to collect all of Richard's newspaper reviews into a kind of omnibus volume."

"You're not making any sense."

He wasn't. He was gibbering.

"Ebsen found out something about Richard."

"From the shotgun microphone?"

"How do you know about that?"

"It doesn't matter, Michael. I know. So what did he find out?"

"You just want to get back at me for Jane, don't you? She told me about your visit this afternoon."

"Jane doesn't have anything to do with this."

"You'd like to see me get blamed for this because you think you'd have a chance for Jane again, don't you? Well, I'll tell you, Tobin, she's in love with me. Deeply in love. So you trying to frame me won't matter. She still won't love you. No matter what you do."

Tobin said, "I want to know why you came here tonight."

"I don't want to tell you."

Tobin reached up and slapped him. He got him square enough and hard enough that the slap had the same effect as a punch. Dailey's head snapped back and he whimpered like a child who'd been kicked.

Dailey surprised him by keeping calm. "You did that because of Jane, didn't you?"

Tobin said, "Maybe."

"She said you're screwed up. Tonight I'm finding out how right she is."

Dailey meant to hurt him and it worked. Hearing your ex-lover's nasty words from the mouth of her new lover is the worst kind of punishment. Tobin sighed, depleted of talk and contrivances.

He turned away from Dailey and went over and picked up the phone. In the moonlit silence, chicken blood and feathers strewn all over, the dial tone was very loud.

"What are you doing?" Dailey said sharply.

"Calling the police."

"Damn you."

"Just shut up, Michael. Please."

He had punched out three digits when Michael came over and grabbed him by the shoulder. "All right," he said, "I'll tell you."

"Then tell me right now. No more bullshit."

"It was the reviews."

"What reviews?"

"The reviews Richard did of Peter Larson's movies."

"What about them?"

"My God, are you really that naive?"

"Don't get pissy with me, Michael. I'm in no mood."

"I need a cigarette." It was, of course, a Gauloises. Filtered.

Tobin drifted back to the phone. "Tell me. Now."

Dailey exhaled smoke pure as frost in the moonlight. "My dear wife Joan *paid* Richard to give Larson's films good reviews."

"Jesus. Payola."

"Exactly. Richard gave them good reviews in all his newspaper pieces and on the TV show."

"So why was he killed?"

Dailey shrugged. Had some more of his French cigarette. "I'm afraid I don't know."

"Why are you here?"

"If the publishing company ever gets wind of the fact that Richard sold his influence, the book project will be off. I came here because our dead friend over there called me tonight and said he knew all about the reviews and wanted three thousand cash."

"Three must have been his lucky number."

"Why?"

"That's what he wanted from me. Three thousand. I brought my checkbook."

From inside his dazzling coat, Dailey took a white envelope. "I brought cash."

"I want to see your gun."

"Why?"

"To see if it's been fired."

"For God's sake, you don't still think I killed Ebsen, do you?"

"Maybe."

"I'm a creature of restaurants and salons, Tobin. Not this."

"The gun."

He held it, smelled it, handled it, without quite knowing what he was looking for. The gun didn't smell as if it had been fired recently. He handed it back. "What's this all about?"

"The gun?"

Tobin nodded.

"I don't usually come into neighborhoods like this one alone."

"Did you find anything?"

"The tapes?"

"Right."

"No."

Tobin thought of the cabbie. Waiting. And most likely wondering. "Have you looked around?"

"Everywhere."

"Damn."

"Why?"

"Because I don't have time to look for myself."

"Why?"

"Because I've got a cab waiting."

"Oh, Christ, I forgot about you and cabs."

"And he's going to be getting damned curious about what's going on in here. I'd better get out of here. The police are going to find out about this soon enough."

Dailey said, "You know that we wish you the best."

"We, Michael?"

"Jane and I."

"Oh. Yes. Sure."

"We do. I mean, in case you were being sarcastic. And I hope you wish us the best, too."

Tobin sighed. "Michael, don't ask me to be good-hearted at the moment, all right?"

He had just taken what he hoped was his final morbid look at Ebsen's corpse and was getting ready to head back outdoors, when the phone rang.

For three rings Tobin and Dailey just stood by the phone and stared at it. Then Tobin went to the phone, putting a finger over his mouth to shush Dailey.

Tobin lifted the receiver, said nothing.

"Did you get the money?"

Now he knew what it was like to be in the electric chair. At the moment the man threw the switch.

He recognized the voice. Of all the voices in the world, why did it have to be this one?

Again, "Did you get the money?" Then, "Damn, Ebsen, are you playing games or what?"

Then, "Shit, that isn't you, is it, Ebsen?"

Then the line went dead.

"Who was it?" Dailey asked.

"Nobody important," Tobin said.

Five minutes later he was in the back seat of the cab giving directions.

24 1:47 A.M.
Tobin stopped at an outdoor phone booth and called his answering service and had the woman look up a certain address in the phone book.

By cab he was half an hour away. When he arrived he found himself on the fringe of Soho. The building he wanted was a two-story warehouse that had been

143

converted to apartments, as had most of the other buildings surrounding it. There was one difference. The windows of the building he wanted glowed with light and music and laughter. Party.

When he reached the front door, he saw that there was an entranceway inside, so he tried the doorknob and walked straight in. A couple was entangled just outside an apartment door, the party furious inside. Tobin envied them. It was always fun at parties to stand in the hall and neck. Over the man's shoulder the woman's eyes opened and crinkled a smile at Tobin in recognition. The party had probably just been upgraded from B to A with the arrival of a small-time celebrity.

She pulled away from her boyfriend. "Look. It's him."

Her boyfriend, obviously not much giving a damn who anybody was at the moment, turned angrily around and said, "Whoop—fucking—ee."

"Don't you know who he is?"

"Of course I do. Now ask me if I give a shit."

"I'm sorry to disturb you," Tobin said.

"Then leave," the boyfriend said. He was trying awfully hard to look like a beach bum who'd been washed up on chill Atlantic shores. He wore an eye-punishing Hawaiian shirt so he could show off all his chest hair and his biceps.

Tobin looked at the woman. "Does Marcie Pierce live here?"

"Upstairs. But I'm not sure she's home. I thought I saw her go out a few minutes ago."

"How about her mother. Is she home?"

The woman seemed confused. "Her mother? Marcie lives alone. Are you sure this is the right Marcie?"

"From Hunter? A film student?"

"Yes, that's Marcie."

"But her mother doesn't live with her?"

The boyfriend decided to put his hands on his hips and have a go at looking threatening. "That's about enough."

Tobin was ready. His blood and his brain were about to transform him into "Yosemite Sam." The guy who took a punch at his partner. The guy who dragged his motorcycle up five flights of stairs to a party. The guy who pushed a dishwasher downstairs. Hitting Michael earlier tonight had felt wonderfully good. But it had only been a slap, and slaps rendered only so much satisfaction. This asshole would render a great deal of satisfaction. Tobin knew the guy would eventually beat his head in, but Tobin would have a great time losing.

The girlfriend wisely set herself between the two men. "Marcie's parents died in a car accident when she was fifteen. She's lived alone since then."

"Oh. I see."

"Is that all?"

Tobin smiled at the woman. "You seem like a pretty decent woman. You could do a lot better than this jerk."

She had to hold back her boyfriend till Tobin got out of the door. "I really like your show," she called as he hit the cold again. "Merry Christmas."

25 2:28 A.M.

The first person he met at Hunter was a security guard who could have doubled as a villian in a pro wrestling setup. "I can't let you in," he told Tobin.

Tobin said, "I'll be up-front with you, all right?"

The guy stood there fifty pounds overweight in his uniform, just outside the doors leading to the film department, and said, "All right, but it won't do any good."

"Being up-front, being honest, showing you myself as one human being to another won't do any good?"

"That's right," the guard said.

"You see that?"

The guard angled his head to see what Tobin was nodding at. "What?"

"On the street corner over there."

"The streetlight over there?"

"No. What's on the streetlight."

"The Santy Claus?"

"Right. The Santy Claus."

"What about it?"

"Well, it's that time of year."

"What time of year?"

Tobin hoped he'd never have to go on a game show with this guy as his partner. "It's holiday time. Giving time. Helping-each-other-out time."

"Oh. Yeah."

"So how about helping me out?"

"Why should I?"

"Because I'm in some trouble and I've got a feeling that somebody who helped get me in trouble is inside that building."

"Then why don't you call the police?"

"Because they won't believe me. They don't give a damn about it being that time of year when people help each other out."

"I don't either."

"Well, you were right."

"I was?"

"Yeah. You said that even if I was up-front with you,

even if I showed you myself as one human being to another, it wouldn't do any good."

"At least I didn't lie."

So Tobin took out his wallet and said, "I suppose you'd get pissed off if I offered you a bribe."

"Like you said, it's that time of year when people help each other out," the guard said.

Tobin knew the guy was going to go call the police, then deny that he'd ever let Tobin in, and certainly deny that he'd taken a bribe. He had to move quickly.

His footsteps were hollow echoing down the dark halls. He could smell cleaning solvent. Moonlight fell in tiny amoeba shapes on the floor. He turned several corners, his breathing ragged, his face covered with sweat. He could still hear her voice on the phone. He had been so stupid.

When he reached the corridor leading to the film lab, he moved even faster. Then he was there.

A desk lamp burned in the outer office. He first checked the editing room. Empty. Then he tried all the inner office doors. Locked. He moved to the secretary's desk and consulted her list of room numbers. He found the main production room number and headed there.

Another corridor. Another right angle. He stood in front of the production room, putting his ear to the door. Nothing.

He jerked open the door and stood there looking around. One wall was filled with TV sets used as monitors. Another contained various small tape recorders and three-quarter-inch video cameras. The east wall held small editing tables for both audio and video. This was where he found her.

His first assumption was that she was dead, the way

she was slumped over the recorder. He ran to her and lifted her gently upward. Blood covered one side of her face, but when he touched a finger to her neck he found at least a dim pulse.

He set her down on the floor, took off his topcoat and put it beneath her head for a pillow. Then he went over to the phone and dialed 911.

When he went back to her, he knelt down beside her and for a long moment just stared at her. The older he got, the less able he seemed to judge people. Staring at her now he felt a variety of things for her prettiness—affection, lust, paternalism. But he had been so wrong about her. The virtues he'd attributed to her were fanciful—in his mind only.

But his thoughts made him guilty. She seemed to have only a fragile grip on life, so now was no time to feel sorry for himself at her expense. He said, "Marcie, can you hear me?"

At first he thought he'd imagined the slight flicker of her eyelids. But then her eyes opened.

She was trying. "I'm sorry, Tobin."

"Who hit you?"

"I should never have gotten involved with Ebsen."

"Why did you?"

"He told me how easy it would be to get money. All I had to do was help him edit the tapes. He wasn't a great technician." Then she went "Ooooo" as pain apparently traveled across her head.

"So Ebsen followed people around with his shotgun microphone so he could send them the tapes 'Compliments of Richard Dunphy' and embarrass them?"

"Yes. He taped everybody around but he really hated Dunphy. He was obsessed with him."

He touched her forehead. Stroked it gently. "Why did you lie to me about your mother?"

She swallowed. "I get sentimental at Christmas, I guess." She smiled. "I make myself feel better with fantasies."

Tobin felt a sadness sharp as a weapon pierce his chest. But he had to go on with his questions. "Ebsen found something out about somebody, didn't he?"

"Tobin—" She swallowed again. This time he could see how her throat contracted. "I don't know how much more I can talk."

He knew she wasn't exaggerating. She was suddenly bathed in sweat but her flesh was cold.

"He found out about Dunphy being paid to praise Peter Larson's movies, right?"

"Right."

He shook his head. "Who killed Dunphy?"

"I'm not sure."

"Bullshit." He couldn't control his anger. He thought again of how she'd lied to him.

"I lied about a lot of things, Tobin. But I'm not lying about this. I'm not sure. Ebsen had one tape he sent to somebody but he wouldn't tell me who. He just said if he got the money he wanted, we'd split it. He was really excited. Said he'd stumbled onto somebody who was really going to have to pay. But he still wouldn't tell me. Ebsen liked playing games like that. I wasn't with him the day he—" She grimaced again and made a pained noise.

"Who hit you tonight?"

"Stay right there," the guard said from the doorway.

Tobin looked up and found the man, gun drawn, advancing on him. "Shit," he said, seeing all the blood. He glared at Tobin. "You bastard."

"I didn't hit her."

"Right."

"I've already called nine-one-one."

This seemed to confuse the man. "Oh, yeah?"

"Yeah."

"Now I have to finish here." He looked back down at Marcie and said, "Who hit you, Marcie?"

"Whoever followed me inside tonight. They must have followed me from my apartment."

"Where you lived with your dead mother who baked you cookies."

"I'm sorry about all the lies, Tobin. I actually did have a mother once."

"Good for you." Tobin was getting as sweaty as Marcie. He saw his chances for finding the real killer slipping away. He thought of his list and the names on it but none of them seemed likely suspects at the moment. "Do you remember the day Ebsen told you about the special tape?"

"Yeah. Sort of. Why?"

"Do you remember who he was following that day?"

From down the hall came thunderous pounding. Obviously the ambulance had arrived. The guard, looking as if he still wanted to have a public hanging with Tobin as the hangee, said, "I'll go see who that is." Who did he think it was going to be—Domino's Pizza?

When he'd left, Tobin said, "Please, think, Marcie. Who was he following around that day he got so excited?"

She thought. "No—" Then she frowned in what seemed part pain and part concentration. "He just said that this man he was following had more to lose than even Dunphy."

Tobin was thinking about Michael Dailey and his book contract when an ambulance team dressed in white and the fog of the winter night came rushing through the door.

They pushed Tobin aside as they got Marcie ready for the gurney.

Tobin knew he had to get out of here before the guard came back or the man would hold him for the police. He went over to Marcie and said, "Did he get the tape tonight?"

She was on the gurney, strapped in. "No. Because I didn't even know what he was looking for. He hit me and panicked and ran."

"Without the tape?"

She nodded, then grimaced. "Without the tape."

"And you didn't recognize his voice?"

"He kept a handkerchief over his face. I couldn't even see him really."

One of the ambulance men, irritated at how close Tobin was standing, said, "Would you mind moving back, buddy?"

Then Tobin left, into the shadows of the corridor, out one of the side doors to the street, sneaking up in back of his waiting cab.

By now he knew, of course. Knew well and sadly.

He gave the driver an address and sat back, trying to figure out how he was going to handle it. On the way over he made a single stop, a phone booth. He was getting as good at phone-boothing as Clark Kent. Huggins didn't seem at all happy to hear from him. Even less happy about having to get out of bed. Huggins said, "Tomorrow's Christmas Eve."

"Then you'll want to get an early start on the day. You've probably got a lot of shopping left to do."

Tobin hung up and got back in his cab and went back across the cold city.

26 3:27 A.M.

There were still lights shining from the second floor when Tobin's cab pulled up. This time he paid off the driver and sent him away.

The security guard recognized him and even offered a little sort of salute. Tobin tried to return the gesture but he couldn't, quite. Maybe it was because he didn't like saluting, but more probably it was because of what lay ahead of him. Now that he knew whom he was looking for, he'd almost rather not know.

The elevator didn't take long enough getting him to the second floor. When he stepped out into the reception area he saw that all that remained of the party now was the debris—a depressing spectacle of streamers that had crashed to earth, confetti that looked like colorful vomit, plastic glasses filled with the dregs of drinks and floating cigarette butts to give the liquid the color of urine samples. Smoke choked the air. Perfumes mixed too sweetly. But there was something else odd, too—the complete lack of humanity. This might have been one of those *Twilight Zone* shows about the last man on earth: He finds everything set up for a party but nobody to share it with.

Then a voice said, "You know, don't you, Tobin?"

He turned and saw Frank Emory leaning against a filing cabinet, a drink tilted precariously in his hand.

152

Frank looked as if he'd been partying for a week and had forgotten to sleep.

"Yeah," Tobin said, "I know." He shook his head. "You sat in your office and told me you were a failure—even though you'd already sold your company. When I found that out, I started thinking."

"I really wouldn't have let them arrest you."

"I'll take your word for that."

Frank had some of his drink. Then he set it down calmly on the filing cabinet and scratched his beard-stubbled chin. "I really do give a damn about you; have I ever told you that?"

"Yeah, you've told me that, Frank."

"But I was in a bind."

"I'll grant you that, Frank. You were in a bind. A big one."

"So I didn't have a lot of choice."

Tobin shook his head, hating Frank and pitying him at the same time. "Richard was killed because you were afraid that if the company that was going to buy you out found that Richard was taking payola, the deal would be off, right?"

Quietly, Frank said, "Right." Then he flung his arm dramatically around the room. "You know what my oldest son says when he thinks something's neat?"

"What does he say, Frank?"

"He says 'bitchin'. As in 'That's a 'bitchin' car' or 'That's a bitchin' movie.' Well, you know what, Tobin?"

"What?"

"Tonight we had one bitchin' good party here. You know that?"

"I'm happy for you, Frank."

Frank eyed him as soberly as he could. "I really do give a damn about you, Tobin. I really do."

"Ebsen had to be killed, too."

"Ebsen." This time when Frank waved his hand it was with a sense of dismissal. "He was really slime. He was trying to blackmail Dunphy for stealing his script—which Dunphy *did*, in fact—but then he followed him around with one of those goddamn shotgun microphones and that's how he found out Dunphy was taking bribes."

"Two people, Frank. Killed. Jesus." He was exhausted.

Frank sort of hugged the filing cabinet. Sort of put his face down on it.

"I'm sorry, Tobin."

"For what?"

Frank's head rose and he looked at Tobin. "For what? What the hell are you talking about? I'm sorry I killed Richard and even that slimy bastard Ebsen." This was the most animated he'd been since Tobin had entered the office. "I killed them and I'm going to have to pay for it."

Gently, Tobin said, "You didn't kill them, Frank."

"What the hell are you talking about? Of course I did."

"Frank, I know you very well—remember?"

"What's that supposed to mean?"

"It means you don't have what it takes to kill somebody."

"Oh, sure, I see what you're saying. Old wishy-washy Frank Emory. He doesn't have the *balls* to kill anybody. That's what you mean, isn't it, Tobin? That's what you goddamn mean, isn't it?"

"Yes, Frank, that's what I mean."

"Well, you're wrong. I not only killed one person, I killed *two*. Two fucking people, Tobin, do you understand that?"

"Where is she, Frank?"

154

"Who?"

"Dorothy."

"What the hell's Dorothy got to do with this?"

"You don't have the balls, Frank, but Dorothy does."

From behind him a female voice said, "I'm going to take that as a compliment, Tobin."

Dorothy had come out from one of the darkened offices. She looked remarkably fresh, even lovely.

"You like a drink, Tobin?" she said.

"Yes," he said. "Yes, I would."

"Scotch all right?"

"Scotch is fine."

She went over to the bar and poured the three of them healthy doses of Scotch, then brought them over. She'd put on perfume recently and as she brushed close to him the smell of it was erotic.

She stood next to Frank and said, "The funny thing was, I didn't have to kill either of them."

"Why not?" Tobin said.

"You remember seeing me the night Richard was killed?"

"Downstairs, when I was telling Frank he should go have an IRA cocktail?"

"Exactly."

"What about it?"

"Well, do you remember one of the grips came up and said Frank had a phone call?"

"Yes."

"Well, the phone call was from Frank's lawyer. The papers had just been signed."

"God," Tobin said. "So no matter what came out in the press about Richard taking bribes—"

She laughed. He could hear the shock and panic and terror in the sound. "Yes. But I went into his dressing room without knowing that the deal had been signed

155

and killed him. For absolutely no good reason at all. Frank and I were already off the hook as far as the company goes."

She finished her Scotch in a gulp. "I think I need a little more."

Tobin followed her to the bar. Everything there looked sad and depressing. Mashed-up paper cups and cigarette butts everywhere, and various kinds of dips smeared all over the once-white tablecloth.

"But Ebsen you had to kill," Tobin said.

"You want some more?"

She held up the bottle.

Tobin shook his head.

She filled half her glass.

"But you had to kill Ebsen, right?" he repeated.

"As it turned out, yes. He knew everything. He'd just keep on blackmailing us, only now murder would be in the bargain." She sighed. "He knew that one of us had killed Dunphy. We were the only ones who had reason to."

She took another jolt of her drink and then her eyes roamed to Frank and she said, "The past four months have been terrible. I just wanted things to be as they used to be." She smiled. "I was even trying to be nicer to Frank."

Tobin said, "I never could decide."

"Decide what?"

"If I liked you or not."

She looked at him without coyness and said, "You've come to a decision?"

"I admire your courage. Even if you did it, Dorothy."

"I didn't have any choice. Anyway, admiring my courage isn't the same as liking me."

Tobin laughed without quite knowing why. "No, I guess it isn't."

156

Then he saw that she was looking past him and she said, "For God's sake, Frank."

Tobin turned.

Frank stood there looking more drunk and disheveled than ever. Except now he had a chrome-plated .45 in his hand.

"Frank, just what do you plan to do with that?" Dorothy asked.

"Kill Tobin if I need to."

"That's brilliant. That would really help us out. Anyway, he's the best friend you've ever had."

"I don't mean I'd kill you out of any kind of malice or anything, Tobin."

Tobin said, "No, I often kill people I like."

"Well, goddammit!" Frank shouted. "I've got to do some goddamn thing, don't I?"

And suddenly tears filled his eyes and his voice became tight with grief. "She killed two people—for me! Because I didn't have the courage to do what I needed to do!" He slammed the fist without the gun hard into the edge of the filing cabinet.

And then he screamed.

From the force and angle with which he'd struck the cabinet, Tobin assumed that he'd broken a knuckle or two, if not the wrist.

Dorothy went to him. She held out her hand and said, "Now quit being stupid, Frank, and give me the gun."

When he complied, she took it and handed it to Tobin. "Now go over there and sit in that chair, Frank, and let's have a look at that hand. You're such a goddamn *child*, Frank. You really are."

As she guided her husband to the chair, she looked back at Tobin and said, "Call the police, all right?"

"You sure?"

She thought a moment and then she said, "Yes, Tobin, I'm sure."

Tobin said, "You know what?"

"What?"

He smiled. "I do like you, after all."

Then he went and called the cops.

27 8:49 P.M.

"You know what kind of dumb son of a bitch this Huggins is?" Neely said.

He was telling the story for maybe the thirty-eighth time that night. It was apparently the sort of story the people at Diablo's liked because everybody who heard it laughed. A lot.

"So Tobin here is standing there talking to Huggins—and this is right in front of the fucking Brill Building—and I'm right behind him toking on a joint. This is broad fucking daylight! Can you believe how dumb cops are?"

Tobin wasn't sure why he'd let Neely drag him along (Neely wanted to celebrate "our" victory, being of the mind apparently that he'd played some key role in getting Tobin free), but he really didn't, this Christmas Eve, have anyplace else to go. He'd spent four hours with his kids this afternoon and given them their presents and given them more kisses than either one of them wanted—and at one point he'd started crying and hugging them and laughing all at the same time, and he knew they had to be wondering how stable old Pops really was—and now he didn't have anything left to do but sit here in Diablo's and get smashed and listen to Neely tell his story for the thirty-ninth time about what morons cops were (when in fact they weren't) and how he'd outsmarted them (when in fact he hadn't).

Tobin spent part of a drink thinking about Jane Dunphy, whom he'd called and who'd told him that she and Michael were "escaping to Tahiti," and about Peter Larson, who was going to be charged with coercion.

There was a Tony Bennett ballad on the jukebox suddenly—"Green Dolphin Street," the definitive version with the Ralph Sharon trio—and suddenly Tobin, tired of Neely and the laughers, looked around for the sad skinny woman he'd seen earlier. She had enough Christmas jazz on her body to pass for a holiday tree. But at the moment he didn't give a damn. He just went down to the end of the bar where she sat alone like a sentry guarding loneliness.

"Hi," he said.

"Hi." Then she saw who he was and said, "Oh, you're—"

"It doesn't matter. How about dancing with me?"

She was plain and now she was nervous. "You want to dance with *me*? Really?"

"Please," he said, "please." And he knew he was getting the way he'd been this afternoon with his kids, with that kind of overwhelming sadness, a distinct sense of pleading in his voice.

So then she stood up and they went out on the dance floor and he took her in his arms, and if he'd ever held a woman tighter, he couldn't remember when it had been.

"Gee," she said. "You're not at all like I expected."

He smiled at her and brought her even closer so that her perfume filled his senses and gave him an odd sort of peace. "No," he said. "People never are what you expect, are they?"